The earl gave Angella credit for spunk, but was she truly innocent?

A moment later he pulled her roughly into his arms.

She gasped, first melting against him, then stiffening in anger. She struggled in the earl's arms. "Let me go, you odious blackguard. You're…you're as dreadful as the dastardly vicar!" Then she burst into tears.

The earl, who until that moment had taken the whole incident rather lightly, had taken her into his arms to test her reaction to his attentions. At her response, guilt curled around his heart. He couldn't remember when he'd last felt so awkward around a woman, for indeed the woman he'd held close to him was not a child. Her body, though thin, was the body of a maturing young woman.

Holding her, he was at a loss how to comfort her, how to still the tempest of her tears or how to apologize. He did not need to be told his cynical actions had ripped away the last shreds of her dignity and self-control.

For a long time she wept, not seeming to realize he held her lightly in his embrace.

Books by Carolyn R. Scheidies

Love Inspired Heartsong Presents

A Proper Guardian
The Earl's Ward

CAROLYN R. SCHEIDIES

Carolyn's publishing credits include over two dozen books, both fiction and nonfiction, several of which have garnered awards. She's written for a variety of publications, has a regular newspaper column and has worked as an editor, speaker/teacher and book reviewer. Scheidies lectured at the University of Nebraska at Kearney for several years. She speaks to different groups, leads workshops and now teaches adult enrichment writing classes at Central Community College. Key to her writing is hope. She wants her writing to draw others to know the love and hope that only Jesus Christ can provide.

CAROLYN R. SCHEIDIES

The Earl's Ward

HEARTSONG
PRESENTS

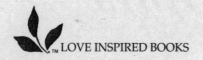

LOVE INSPIRED BOOKS

Recycling programs
for this product may
not exist in your area.

ISBN-13: 978-0-373-48676-2

THE EARL'S WARD

Copyright © 2013 by Carolyn R. Scheidies

www.Harlequin.com

Printed in U.S.A.

Fear thou not; for I am with thee: be not dismayed;
for I am thy God: I will strengthen thee; yea, I will
help thee; yea, I will uphold thee with the right
hand of my righteousness.

—*Isaiah* 41:10

Sometimes life throws a curve and we feel all alone.
Yet, God isn't blindsided by circumstances beyond
our control. If we look back, we'll see how God
put others into our lives just at the right time.
I am thankful that when I've felt alone, God has
always sent dear friends and family members to
remind me that He is there and that He cares.
While I have many friends, I dedicate this book to
one special friend who has walked with me through
good times and bad since college days.

God bless you, Gloria Geiselman, and thanks.

Chapter 1

With dainty white hands, Angella Denning smoothed her worn gown, which hung limply from her frame. It had not been new for several years and even then had been painstakingly sewn of cheap material by her mother. Economies were always necessary on her father's meager living, not to mention his generosity with what little they had. The dress had fit once upon a time, before she lost two of the most important people in her life—her dear beloved parents.

When her father, the Reverend Andrew Denning, died of fever after ministering in the village unstintingly for the past ten years, the folks of the small village mourned with her grieving mother. When her mother died soon after of the same fever, Angella was allowed to stay until a new vicar was chosen. There was no place for her to go. No one offered to help, though she would gladly have worked for her board and room—not that she could do much.

Slight of stature, she was no match for the women who toiled all day in the fields or who worked at the Big House, as the Lucashire family residence was known. It was from the Lucashire family the vicar received his living. Not that anyone had so much as glimpsed the young earl since the death of the kindly old peer—his father.

The shopkeeper told her, "The new earl is not cut from the same cloth as his good father." Seldom in residence, he cut his dash in London. The village maidens squealed as they gossiped about the rakish antics of the young lord. Angella was disgusted. She had no use for men who refused to take their responsibilities to their people seriously.

Yet, on her deathbed, her mother made her promise to contact the earl if her grandfather would not have her, but she knew not how. No one wanted to take a message to the Big House. She doubted the profligate earl would wish to take as his ward some unfledged chit.

After her mother's death, she sent off a missive to her maternal grandfather, the Marquess of Monforg. It had been returned unopened like all the other missives sent to Monforg castle throughout the years. Angella knew her mother's story by heart. When her mother, the marquess's only daughter, defied him by marrying a "no-account" parson, he cut her off without a farthing. He never even acknowledged the existence of Angella or her older brother, Edward.

Angella expected nothing less than another rejection from the starched-up peer. It pained her that her grandfather did not care—not for his daughter or his grandchildren. Still, she had to make one final attempt. She'd promised her mother.

If only Edward was not so far away. She had also posted a letter to Edward, but there had scarcely been time for it to reach him in India and for him to return home. Besides, as he had told them in his infrequent letters, he was often far from the missionary compound.

Thus, Angella had no place to go and no money with which to travel, even if she did know where to go. From the empty flagpole others reported viewing at Lucashire Hall, Angella knew the earl was not in residence. Who knew when he would return!

When the new vicar first arrived, he had sympathized with her plight—or so she'd thought. At the time, she had been grateful when he'd told her with a strange smile, "You may stay at the vicarage, Miss Denning, for now."

While the situation made her uncomfortable, the vicar was old enough to be her guardian and the housekeeper did live there, too. How could she have guessed the man was not the honorable man of God her father was?

He thundered from the pulpit like some Old Testament prophet, but comported himself like some monster in his own home. He covered it well with his sanctimonious arrogance. Not even Mrs. Marsh, the elderly homebound woman who so loved Angella's mother, believed her hints that all was not well.

Never had a man frightened her as did the vicar. His son was a different matter. His cries drew her to the parlor when she found the vicar beating the child. "Stop! Stop!" She tried to grab the bloodied whip. Andrew, whose shirt hung in tatters from the whipping, stared up at her with frightened, glazed eyes.

"No, Miss Denning. Leave me be… I…can take it." The fear she witnessed in his eyes was for her. Staring into the face of his father, she understood. There was a strange glitter in the vicar's gaze as he held her at bay. He licked his thick lips in a way that sent chills down her spine.

"This is between me and my son. The boy incurred my wrath, and he shall be punished." There was no anger, only a deep gratification in the man's face as he eyed the object of torture.

"He's just a boy and he is your son. He's bleeding. Isn't that enough?" She'd intended to sound forceful, but the words came out breathless, frightened.

He noticed, and a slow dreadful smile stretched his mouth. "He is mine. I do what I will with what is mine, and I expect complete obedience. Just as it says in God's Word—*Honor thy father and mother*—which is the first commandment with promise. You'll understand…in time."

Her dark green eyes narrowed. "It also says in Ephesians 6:4, *And, ye fathers, provoke not your children to wrath: but bring them up in the nurture and admonition of the Lord.*"

The vicar's cheeks puffed out. His eyes reddened. "How dare you question the way I raise my son."

"I know God is a God of love. You know nothing of love." Though her insides quailed, Angella was not about to back down.

"I don't, do I?" His gaze roved her worn gown.

Crossing her arms over her bosom, she blushed. "That, Reverend, is not love and you well know it."

"We'll see about that," he growled. "One of these days you'll be grateful to me."

Angella felt like the terrified rabbit she'd once seen caught in a snare in the wood. She had nowhere to go and no one to whom she could turn. *Lord, show me what to do.*

As much as she would have liked to help the boy, she knew the man would never allow her, nor anyone else, to stand in his way. If he desired to beat his son, as he had several times the past month, she would not be able to stop him.

Then at dinner that evening when the vicar turned his attention toward her, she quailed. After dismissing his son from the table, the vicar made a pompous pronouncement. "I think you would make a suitable wife."

Her utensil clattered onto the plate, her hunger forgotten. She had not seen this coming.

"I do not think so," she managed to say, trying not to tremble.

A slow, cruel smile played over his face. "Oh, my dear, by now the good people of the village will expect an announcement."

"How can that be? I am in your care. Nothing more."

"A nubile young woman and a virile, unrelated man in the same household? Think on it." His gaze held hers.

Leaning away, Angella felt the back of the chair. Should she tell the truth? "I don't much care for your ways."

He reached for her hand, then frowned when she pulled away. "That matters not. You have no other options…do you?"

"I cannot. I…" She clutched her hands as fear settled deep inside her.

"Think on this tonight. I expect an answer on the morrow." With that, he finished his meal and left her staring at her plate and praying.

Her prayers for deliverance seemed to reach no higher than the ceiling of her small bedchamber where she had once felt so safe and secure. Not long past, the vicarage seemed like a haven. Now it closed in around her like a prison and her own room a trap with no escape.

Her only comfort was the helpless black kitten she had rescued from the cruelties of the village lads and now held against her cheek. Its soft purr soothed something within.

After she retired, the vicar himself entered her bedchamber, looking for all the world as though he owned it. As indeed he did; at least, he had the right of it for as long as he held the vicarship.

"What? How dare you!" Angella pulled up the coverlet to cover her thin, worn nightgown. "Get out!" The kitten hissed.

He merely laughed, his eyes glittering. "Just wanted to tell you this is your last night alone."

"What, no engagement period?"

"No time, my dear, when you already reside with me."

She realized he sensed her feeling of entrapment and smiled. "I require your hand in the morning."

"If I give it not?" Anger spurred her words.

His eyes roved over her slight form. "There are ways to make you see the light. 'Tis not seemly for a young maiden to live under the same roof with an unmarried man without a proper chaperone. This you well know. Who knows what has gone on between us?"

Angella blanched. "Nothing. Nothing at all! The housekeeper…"

"Not enough, and you know it. Besides, who's to take your word in this over mine? I am their spiritual leader." Again she heard the chuckle that so chilled her.

"It will set you down, as well."

He hovered over her. "I think not, my dear, not when I'm finished with my story."

Angella clutched the covers to her even more tightly. "Get out! If the people knew what a scoundrel you are, you'd soon be given your walking papers."

His rotund middle bounced as he laughed. "Who is going to notify His Lordship?" Again he flashed his knowing smile. "He cares little about his estate or the living of a mere vicar, not when his own activities would not bear looking in to."

From the tittle-tattle in the village, Angella knew this to be the case and her heart sank. "When he returns home, I will go to him myself like mother wanted."

"At least I offer you wedded bliss. His Lordship would not offer even that. Leastways, not to his light-skirts."

At that moment, her kitten leaped on the vicar's arm, scratching a trail as the man tried to dislodge the determined animal. Angella grabbed the kitten to her chest, fearing the man's reprisal. "That cat is evil personified."

"No, you are. Now, get out!" With a growl, the vicar left and Angella sensed the kitten's defense had saved her in a way she didn't even want to contemplate.

Angella got up and dragged her dresser in front of the door so there would be no more intrusions that night. Even so, sleep was a long time coming—what there was of it.

The next morning, the vicar's gaze took in her pale face with satisfaction. "Miss Denning."

Angella tensed, noticing the vicar's eight-year-old son did the same, his eyes furtively following his father. Father and son shared the same blond hair, the same washed-out blue eyes. The resemblance ended there. For, Andrew was, at least in the absence of his father, a naturally bright and loving child. In the vicar's presence, he grew silent, watchful, hesitant.

"Miss Denning." The vile man forced cheerfulness as he sat in a chair at the round oak dining table. He waited while the maidservant served him a hearty repast of ham, kippers, hot toast with fresh farm jam and eggs. Just watching the assortment and quantity of food the vicar consumed made Angella's stomach churn.

As the maid left them, he smirked at Angella. "I gave you leave until this morning to make your decision." He looked her up and down until Angella crossed her arms in front of her before dropping them, once more, to her lap. "Truth to tell, there is no decision to make. You have no choice but to accept my generous offer."

His arrogance angered her, and she clenched her hands together under the table. The dreadful man smiled at her. "I have the special license." His son looked at her hopefully, but Angella could not give him hope.

Had not her father said the Lord would never desert her? That He would always be with her no matter what if she but followed His way? Remembering her loving, caring father gave her courage. Angella held her head high. "I don't believe in slavery."

A white ring formed about the vicar's tight lips. "You have good bloodlines—on your mother's side. I'm offering you a place as my wife. I am no lowly parson like your father, willing to glean an existence among the rustics. Not for long. In time, I will have a good and prosperous living—mayhap even in London."

"While you lead one and all to destruction."

Angella did not know why she was being so perverse. It could not help the situation.

"I'd no more marry you than I would a snake." Angella's wrath erupted without recall. Too long she had bottled up her feelings, too long she held them in. Anger mixed with grief and hurt.

He studied her resolute face. There was no hint of softness in the gaze that held his. His hands curled as though around his whip.

Seeing the movement, Angella swallowed the bile in her throat. "Beat me if you will, but it will look suspicious when I cannot drag myself to the altar."

His eyes narrowed dangerously. "I see. Your mind is made up then."

Angella nodded, her chin quivering only slightly. He saw, and smiled that smile that chilled her spine. "You shall regret turning me down. After all, you're hardly top drawer. Think you I cannot find some comely piece to accept what I offer."

Angella snorted. "Fine. I certainly have no intention of toadying to you. I'd rather die than wed you."

"You will wish you had soon enough."

He'd lost no time in gathering the elders. Garbed in his sober black cloak, the vicar stood in front of the church building. His voice boomed out over the village people gathered at his summons. Curiosity showed on their faces and several whispered their suspicions as to the reason for the impromptu meeting.

"I regret having to call this meeting," he told them.

From inside the church where he'd dragged her a few minutes earlier, Angella listened, prayed and wondered.

"As you are aware, Miss Angella Denning has grown up in this community, and all of you know of her good and decent parents. You also know how she insisted on staying on in the vicarage even after I arrived to take up my office."

Denial trembled on Angella's well-shaped lips. How easily he twisted the truth. But what could she say to overset the image of her the vicar left on the minds of those who trusted him?

"I have made her an offer of marriage. And now, as much as it pains me," he continued, his face a study in despair, "I must withdraw my offer. I assumed her to be, as Reverend Denning's daughter, of high moral character and above reproach. How I dislike adding to your burden, for I know that you, as well as I, have cared for the girl." He lowered his voice.

"I fear the deaths of her mother and father, one so soon after the other, has—" he sighed deeply before continuing "—unhinged her mind. She has, on occasion, acted, shall we say, rather forward in our relationship. As difficult as this is to say or to believe, Miss Angella Denning even last night entertained my presence in her bedroom. I thought she had injured herself. Of course as soon as I realized what she was about, I left!"

"What a whisker." Angella groaned, her gaze shifting from the face of the vicar to the villagers and back again. *Lord, stop him. He's mesmerizing them. How can he say such things?* Her heart sank. "How can they believe such things?" she whispered to herself. From the nods, first reluctant, then more sure, she knew he was convincing them of her supposed misdeeds.

By noon the villagers were convinced, totally and completely, of her fall from grace. No one asked for her side of the story. When she would have gone to Mrs. Marsh, who had not been part of the crowd attending the vicar's slanderous speech, the vicar kept her captive, locking her in her room. His forcefulness as he grabbed her arm and hauled her back to the house twisted her knee, but Angella refused to let a sound pass her lips. He would only enjoy her pain.

Later, after the leaders of the village conferred with the vicar, the villagers once more convened in front of the heavy church doors. The vicar forced her to accompany him. Knowing that fighting the minister only gave credence to his lies, she went quietly, the little kitten clinging to her arm.

As she stood beside the vicar on the top step of the church, the leaders called out, "Angella Denning, do you renounce the evil one?"

"Of course I do. I belong to the Lord of creation." Lifting her head, she stared directly into the faces of her accusers.

Discomfited, they glanced away. She heard them murmuring to one another and knew her boldness scored highly. Her nemesis growled. "Ah, but who does she consider the lord of all? The lord of the deep, that's who. Is not the evil one himself the father of distortion and lies?"

His words turned the crowd back. The smithy stepped forward. "Are you a proper Christian?"

"I am. By the name of Jesus Christ…"

The vicar interrupted, "Hear that? She blasphemes.

Look at her clutching the black cat that actually attacked me—without provocation, I might add."

"Aye. Look. Look! And she is a wanton woman, she is."

Another bogus charge. At the unfamiliar voice, Angella peered into the crowd and found the face of a stranger. No doubt put up to his antics by the vicar. Angella's insides churned with disgust—and fear.

When she protested her innocence again and again, the vicar but smiled. "Have you lived in my home without a chaperone?"

Angella hesitated. "Yes, but…"

"Have you not turned down my legitimate offer of marriage, preferring to remain unmarried but in my household?"

"It's not like that." In bewilderment, Angella glanced around at the people her father had ministered to with such love. "You knew my parents. You know me. How can you believe such things about me? He is the one you must rid yourself of. He came to my bedchamber unannounced last night…" As soon as she uttered the words, Angella knew she had said exactly the wrong thing. She half expected those gathered to stone her there and then.

"See. She reveals herself as wanton!" The cry emanated from the stranger in the back.

Another called out, "We must rid ourselves of evil." The now frightened villagers took up the chant until the noise deafened her. The kitten meowed loudly and clung to Angella, digging in her claws until Angella winced.

A tenant farmer reached for the cat. Pushing away the man's hands, Angella cradled the animal in her arms. "Listen to me," she cried. "Listen." But it was too late. The villagers didn't quiet down until the vicar raised his hands, his voice booming over the crowd.

"Good people. You are to be commended," he told them as they quieted to uneasy silence, "for wanting to rid your village of evil."

Patting her shoulder with an affected fatherly concern that made her shudder, he intoned, "Now, good people. We must not be overly harsh. I think it enough we let her leave without hindrance. But leave she must. We must not let her kind taint our children."

He led her back to the vicarage, where he stopped her from taking more than a small satchel and the cat. He didn't even allow her to take her father's Bible or a cape.

"These possessions properly belong to your brother, Miss Denning," the vicar said with a vengeful twist to his lips. "They will remain safely here until he collects them. How would you carry them anyway?" The vicar watched her, waiting, for what? For Angella to break down?

Clenching her teeth, Angella held back her outrage. "I expect them to be kept well. They will be required when Edward returns. I wrote him, you understand." The vicar stiffened momentarily before regaining his arrogant posture.

"I'm sure your behavior will quite put him out of countenance. Mayhap you wish to change your mind."

"Stuff and feathers, Reverend. You've set the whole village in a spin. Think you now to take back your accusations? I think 'tis a bit late for them to see me as the proper wife for such a fine figure of a man as you."

A muscle in his cheek twitched at her sarcasm. "So you will think, mayhap this very night when you find yourself alone, alone and cold, unless some traveler takes a fancy to you." He seemed to relish the thought.

"At least it won't be you." Angella made the thrust in part to disconcert him, and in part to force her mind from the unpleasant image he presented.

Due to the war with Napoleon, most of the young men had been conscripted into the service. Though the war with the accursed Corsican continued, soldiers were being sent home—many no longer fit for duty.

The country, for which they had fought so valiantly, released them from service without compensation. Many of the soldiers, who fought with such bravery and who returned to a nation that offered them nothing—no jobs and no prospects of any sort—plagued the countryside as beggars and bandits. No one was safe.

What chance had she, a young woman alone and unprotected, against the likes of those dangerous men. "Oh, Lord, protect me. Without You, I have no one." She whispered her desperate plea as the elders and the vicar herded her, as she clutched the kitten, to the edge of the village.

The vicar stared at her, a strange smile on his lips, before he turned away. Most of the others followed him, except for a few of the older children. One or two paused as though to say something, but others tugged them away.

Like some ragged urchin, Angella Denning stood forlornly at the edge of the small village with its one east-west main street bisecting the road going north and south. North led to the desolate inlet sea area of Norfolk called The Wash, and south led east to London. But London was days away, even by coach. At least the good people who ran her out of town had the decency to set her sights south, where there was hope of finding human habitation.

On the outskirts of Little Cambrage, which had been her home for so many years, Angella faced down boys with whom she'd grown up. Anger flared. Had her parents been alive, the ruffians would not have dared to treat her in such a cavalier fashion—but then, what could she expect of offspring of the "good" people who allowed the new vicar to expel her from not only her home, but also the village.

A couple of the rougher boys, the ones her father had disciplined more than once, grinned at her. "So the uppity Miss Angella is not so high and mighty now," said a lanky lad with harsh eyes.

"Tom, I…"

"Don't talk to me," he called. Reaching forward, he slapped her. The kitten clawed him.

Howling, he leaped away, holding his hand. "You saw it. That ill-favored cat is trying to protect her. What more proof do you need?"

Angry tears squeezed out of the corners of Angella's wide eyes. "Lord, help me. Help me!"

Wiping the blood from his hand, Tom grabbed a handful of gravel, tossing it in his hand. "I say we rid ourselves of these two."

The other boys shuffled forward, then back hesitantly. Laughing, Tom lobbed the gravel toward her as though testing her response. The gravel spattered a few inches from her feet, covering her worn shoes with dust. When she did nothing, Tom grew bolder.

Motioning for the others to follow suit, he picked up a rock and threw it straight for her. Large green eyes glistened with angry tears as she ducked away, clutching the kitten to her chest.

She felt the sting of the stone thrown by a half-grown village lad who laughed as she flinched away. Blood trickled from her forehead where it hit. The kitten meowed, but Angella was not about to release her to the tender mercies of the children she herself had so recently known as acquaintances, if not friends.

When she tried to turn away, the village boys surrounded her. Taunting her and calling her unspeakable names, they showered her with gravel and larger stones. More than one bruised her soft white skin. As best she could, Angella tried to shield the kitten.

Angella sighed as despair swept over her. What hope had she of going anywhere if those who should have stood with her could so easily turn their backs? What hope had she of finding anything but scorn for a young woman alone with no means?

Could they not at least have offered her transportation to the next village—they who knew she had little stamina to walk for any distance? The morning's events fagged her out. But for her kitten clutched in her thin arms, she might have given up. That, too, had been part of her difficulties, but Angella was not one to give in easily.

Protecting the kitten momentarily took her mind off her own problems. Now the kitten was the only friend she had…next to God, and He seemed very far off.

A verse rang in her mind, *Fear thou not; for I am with thee: be not dismayed; for I am thy God: I will strength thee; yea, I will help thee; yea, I will uphold thee with the right hand of my righteousness.* Her mind clicked off chapter and verse, Isaiah 41:10.

"Lord, I need You. You promised to protect me. Protect me now. Send someone to help me. Please."

Bitterness sat on her soft lips, so used to smiling.

"Lord, what am I to do? Am I to die here with the stamp of wanton woman upon me?" She wouldn't be the first innocent woman to die after charged for being something she was not, she thought. She recalled the article she once read about Joan of Arc. Four hundred years earlier, at the tender age of seventeen, the French peasant girl became a military leader. In the fifteenth century, she helped establish the rightful king on the French throne.

She had been branded a witch for claiming to hear God speak to her in audible voices and been burned at the stake for it. Yet, she was now considered a saint.

Who would mourn for Angella Denning should she die on the road at the edge of the village in which she had grown up? The verse from Isaiah repeated in her mind.

Again and again, Angella quoted, *"Fear thou not; for I am with thee..."* under her breath as the ruffians taunted her. Another spatter of pebbles showered her, and Angella turned her back. She flinched as they scraped her neck, choked back tears at the laughter.

The sun shone down bright and warm, a soft breeze lifted the hem of her worn blue gown. Voices wafted over the fields along with the clang of metal on metal from the smith, the *clop-clop* of hooves on the narrow road.

It all seemed so normal. But for Angella there was no hope. A larger stone caught her cheek. Brushing away her tears, she turned, a flash of anger straightening her shoulders as, once more, she faced the scornful faces of the village lads.

"Ho there! Enough of that!" At the stern command, the youngsters turned to stone as they faced the austere presence in the phaeton.

Angella raised her gaze to meet the deepest brown eyes she had ever seen. Instinctively, she curtsied gracefully even with the kitten tucked in her arm. To be so caught out was lowering, and yet…

Her tormentors edged away and soon ran back to the village. Glancing at the fleeing boys, Angella smiled. "My thanks, m'lord." She took in his tall figure dressed in the first stare of fashion. A many-caped coat flared out from his broad shoulders, proclaiming him a Corinthian of the first water.

A laconic smile touched the lips of the overpowering peer. "What's this about?"

"'Tis no matter to you, m'lord."

"Fustian, child. I'll decide that." He pulled in the matched bays, which tugged on the bit. "Come on up. Can't hold them much longer."

Angella hesitated. "I know you not."

"The Earl of Lucashire at your service, miss." He bowed cynically. "If you be from the village, 'tis my business indeed."

Nodding, Angella stepped forward. Was this the answer to her prayers?

Angella stopped directly beside the phaeton and stared up into the cynical face of its sole occupant. The earl's penetrating eyes probed deep inside her until Angella felt the earl must know her every thought. 'Twas disconcerting, to say the least. Gulping, she shifted the restless kitten in her arms and held on more tightly to her shabby satchel.

An unexpected pain in her knee caused her to grimace. Reaching out, she steadied herself against the high wheel of the carriage. The shooting pain hit without warning and left her weak.

She well knew lack of sleep and her present distress greatly contributed to her weakness. With detached concern, the earl watched her suffering. "Is it your head?" Reaching into his pocket, he pulled out a linen handkerchief and wiped blood from her cheek.

Blushing, Angella lowered her gaze.

Chapter 2

With some interest, the earl watched the girl's cheeks color. It had been a long time since he had witnessed such innocence.

"You must run home and get that tended to, child." His smile was meant to be reassuring. "I'm sure those lads will not dare bother you again."

"Oh, they'd dare." The young woman glanced up at him, then away. "My parents are dead, m'lord. I've no place to go."

The earl straightened then. "Where were you heading when I came along?"

She shrugged. "I was given no choice but to leave the village." Lifting her trembling chin, she looked at him with regal dignity. Color stayed on her high cheekbones and her sensitive mouth fascinated him. He smiled laconically at the decided spark in her eyes.

"Surely there's someone who will take you in. You did not have to leave."

"Oh, but I did, m'lord. The vicar named in place of Reverend Denning saw to it." Anger flashed against him, darkening her eyes to stormy gray.

The change fascinated him, as her accusation took him aback. "What's this, you say? Reverend Denning gone? I did not know. When did he leave?"

"But, m'lord," she protested. "Don't you know? Reverend Denning d-died." Tears mingled with blood on her face. "Didn't you fill his living?" As the truth hit, she stepped back. "You didn't care enough to fill it yourself, did you? You left that to a hireling."

Under her steady gaze, the man whose penetrating look discomfited others, glanced away. "Well, I... Stuff and nonsense, child. I was busy."

"In London, I can imagine." Her sarcasm was not lost on him. "I trust you cut quite a dash."

Out of countenance with the chit, the earl spat out, "Impertinent chit. You might be grateful to your betters."

"Betters? Grateful?" The girl laughed an unhappy laugh. "'Tis because of you I no longer have a home in the village."

"Me? What poppycock is this?"

"La, 'tis you who allowed the choosing of Reverend Carter," she said, her face hardened at the name, "for the Little Cambrage living. He came a fortnight ago."

"My fault, is it?" Despite himself, he felt curious. Gazing down at her thoughtfully, the earl had his hands full of the prancing horses who were anxious to be off. For a moment he relaxed his grip on the reins. Taking advantage of the earl's momentary lapse, the matched pair pulled forward, unbalancing the girl. With a cry, she toppled. The earl hauled her onto the phaeton beside him. Automatically she clutched the kitten so tightly it meowed in loud protest. Her lightweight satchel swung from her elbow.

"Wha… What!" Her large eyes mirrored her admiration of his rescue as he let the horses move on at a controlled trot. As the horses pranced down the road through the village, the young woman averted her eyes. It seemed as though all activity stopped as they drove past. She shuddered when a multitude of eyes stared at them.

Catching her breath, the young woman inquired, "Where are you taking me?"

"Away from prying eyes," said the earl, taking in the condemning stares of the townsfolk. Whatever could this young thing have done to so raise their ire? Why had the girl not gone off to relatives? And why did she blame him? It bore some investigation. That is, if the chit didn't have bats in her cockloft. He glanced at her averted face; she didn't appear caper-witted.

He recalled his father speaking highly of Reverend Denning. He himself had met him only once or twice. For, between Harrow, Oxford and London, he was seldom home, even on weekends—at least not after the untimely death of his mother. When he did come home, he did not seek the sanctuary of the village church. He was no hypocrite to live one way all week long, then put on a sanctimonious face for Sunday. He had never done so and he despised those who did. He had little use for hypocrites and liars.

He shifted uncomfortably. Of course, that did not include the usual polite flattery that a current flirt expected. That was part and parcel of the game. A rather devious game, he admitted to himself.

Stuff! He was well shot of London and its hypocrisies. At Lucashire he would live as he pleased, bowing to no one, playing no games. Again he glanced at the girl who rode uneasily beside him, her attention on soothing the little black kitten. Obviously the chit was not superstitious, but many still were, even in this enlightened age. Could that cat be part of the girl's problem?

She looked somewhat familiar and he dimly recalled meeting her years before at one of his birthday celebrations. Yes, that was it. With his cousin Betsy when both were scarcely out of leading strings.

Letting the reins slip through his hands, he hurried the horses through the village. As it faded into the distance behind them, the young woman gave a great sigh of relief. The kitten in her lap meowed loudly.

"I know you're hungry, little one, but I can't help that right now." She stroked her soft fur. "At least you're alive."

"I'd like an explanation, child. Why did the good folk of Little Cambrage throw you out?"

Biting her lip, the young woman continued stroking the kitten, which now settled down in her lap and, with a huge yawn for one so tiny, fell asleep. "I suppose you have a right to know, since Mother made me promise to contact you if all else failed."

The earl's eyebrows rose at this startling statement. "I see." But he didn't and she appeared to know it, much to his annoyance.

Mischievously, she glanced over at him. "I doubt

that." She sobered. "You may or may not have guessed, but Reverend Denning was my father."

"Come now. I can hardly credit the villagers turning out a daughter of their beloved pastor."

"They were manipulated. Soon after Mother and Father died, I wrote to my brother, Edward, but—if he received my letter at all—'tis highly unlikely he'd be able to return for some time."

"Why is that?" After their run, the horses trotted along the road, content to be moving ahead.

"He's in India."

"With the military, I suppose." Respect for her brother shone in his eyes, then faded.

"No, as a missionary with William Carey."

"A missionary. You jest. What good can that accomplish?"

"Eternal life for who knows how many natives. They need the Lord, too."

"They have hundreds of gods."

"But no hope," the young woman said with quiet confidence. "We are called to minister to all peoples. I am proud he went."

"Even if it leaves you without a protector?" the earl asked, adding, "Surely there are other relatives."

She shrugged. "There is my mother's father. But, Grandfather, you see, won't recognize me. He was furious when mother married a lowly vicar rather than some starched-up wealthy peer."

"You were told to contact me?"

She sighed. "No one was too helpful in that regard. It might have been different if your father still lived, but you…"

A wry smile touched his lips. "I can guess. They

didn't want you besmirched by contact with a rake such as I."

"Actually I did not know what to do. When Reverend Carter came, I thought he was being kind when he allowed me to stay on. I did not know…" She closed her eyes; her thin shoulders trembled.

"Go on," commanded the earl, but not unkindly. Her words began a chill at what might have transpired.

Haltingly she told her story. For some time the earl did not speak as he fought his rage at what the vicar had done to her. That is, if she was telling the truth and not spinning some Banbury tale to engage his sympathy. He'd discover the truth of the matter soon enough.

"Look at me." She did so and he scrutinized the face with its deep green eyes, straight nose and sensitive mouth. There was a hesitant plea in her eyes he did not miss. Unless she was a much better actress than he gave her credit for being, she believed everything she told him.

"What is your name, Miss Denning?"

"Angella." Her gaze was hopeful.

Great! All he needed was some unfledged chit underfoot.

As though sensing his anger, Angella averted her eyes. "We're well past the village, m'lord. I am sure if you set me down now, no one will bother me."

The earl's eyebrow rose. "What fustian is this? Set you down in this stretch of wilderness. What do you plan to do?"

Angella cringed at his tone. "My affairs need not concern you further. You have no wish to be plagued with some young woman you didn't even know existed fifteen minutes or so ago."

This was so close to what the earl himself was thinking, he stared at her in surprise. "The affair is not of my
making, but if you think I'm going to let some gently
bred child down here, you've an attic to let."

"I am well in possession of my wits, thank you. I'll
have you know I am twenty years and not some child."
Angella glared at her rescuer, obviously stung.

He eyed her speculatively in her threadbare gown.
True her hair, though tangled, was gloriously thick as it
cascaded down her back. He took in her thin arms and
shoulders, a sure sign she had not been eating properly
for some time. There wasn't much of a figure to be seen
under the loose bodice, either.

Pulling the horses to a halt at the roadside under
a thick stand of oak trees, the earl faced the girl who
stared back at him determinedly. He gave her credit for
spunk, but was she truly innocent? A moment later he
pulled her roughly into his arms.

She gasped, first melting against him, then stiffening in anger. She struggled in the earl's arms. "Let me
go, you odious blackguard. You're…you're as dreadful as the dastardly vicar!" Then she burst into tears.

The earl, who until that moment had taken the whole
incident rather lightly, had taken her into his arms to
test her reaction to his attentions. At her response, guilt
curled around his heart. He couldn't remember when
he'd last felt so awkward around a woman, for indeed
the woman he'd held close to him was not a child. Her
body, though slight, was the body of a maturing young
woman.

Holding her, he was at a loss how to comfort her,
how to still the tempest of her tears or how to apologize. He did not need to be told his disparaging actions

had ripped away the last shreds of her dignity and self-control. For a long time she wept, not seeming to realize he held her lightly in his embrace.

When Angella lifted her head, she was surprised to see embarrassment in the earl's eyes. She knew her expression showed astonishment that she had allowed him to hold her after his unexpected embrace. Scooting away from him as far as the narrow seat would allow, she hugged her arms across her chest.

Eyeing the discomfited earl with suspicion, Angella broke the tension first. "I got blood all over your jacket."

With the lightest of touches, he traced the wound on her forehead. "At any rate, I do think this has almost stopped bleeding. Your cheek, too."

Angella tried to smile, but failed. "You may set me down now."

He shook his head. "I shan't hear of it. You're coming with me to Lucashire."

"I don't think so. Not after…" She bit her lip and nervously stroked the cat, who seemed not to have even noticed the tempestuous drama of the past few moments.

The earl's visage darkened. "'Tis not my usual practice to ravish innocent young maidens, especially those under my care."

"Could have fooled me," Angella muttered, but knew the earl heard her. A muscle twitched in his cheek.

His lips curled up at the corners. "'Twas but a simple embrace, and at least we correctly discerned the truth of the matter. You are not a mere child."

"You might have taken my word for that…like a gentleman, but, of course," she said, "I have found them in remarkably short supply since Papa's death." She glared at the earl. She sensed he recognized her anger was mostly a front to cover her humiliation.

"A pretty speech," he retorted, "but the women I know have little use for either veracity or virtue."

Angella stared at him. "You certainly know a strange breed of women."

"Ditto for you and men, I'd say. Now, let's quit fencing. I'm taking you to Lucashire, and that is that."

Angella straightened her shoulders. "No, not unless you can offer me a legitimate position in your household. I'll not sit in your pocket like some missish damsel or worse. You didn't come to the country to play guardian to an impoverished vicar's daughter."

The earl's grip on the reins tightened. "Very perceptive. However, you'll do what I want you to do, Miss Angella Denning. Besides, for what are you fit? Certainly not housework."

She hesitated then, before answering carefully. "I do well at sums. I can keep books. I am a great organizer. I can write up the speeches you give in the House of Lords."

The earl hooted at this. "I vow, child. I haven't but once stepped into those hallowed halls. Think you I spend my time preparing speeches for pompous lords who have no use for an upstart in their midst? Not to mention the time doing so would take from…"

"The baize tables, gambling and other pursuits," ground out Angella. "And here I was thinking you were more than a London dandy. Forgive me."

He frowned at the discerning look Angella gave him from beneath impossibly long lashes. "Now, look here, Miss Denning. There are some good men running this country."

"Yes, and many others who should take up their proper responsibilities."

"Be that as it may," the earl agreed, continuing, "what would an unfledged chit know about running England? I daresay the House of Lords is beyond your ken to comprehend."

"Is it now?" Angella's eyes narrowed at his challenge. "Who is going to run this country if younger men refuse to take their God-given responsibilities seriously? M'lord, farmers are rising up in riots, the corn laws are ridiculously unfair, farmers are fighting for their existence. What will happen to the expanded farms once the war ends and their products are no longer required? People are starving. English people. Don't you care?" She took in a deep breath. "What would you know of starving while you sit at tables overflowing with food that would feed a normal family for months?"

The earl glared at Angella. "Who are you? I've not known a woman like you before."

He frowned when Angella told him, "I imagine your experiences with women seldom have gone deeper than paying for numerous fripperies, not discussing affairs of state. Am I correct?"

The girl's question gave him pause. In drowning his guilt in riotous living, he'd done more than neglect his responsibilities to his estate. Not, he defended himself, that he hadn't been involved in decisions. Except for one or two, he amended, thinking of the new vicar.

She continued, "And what about the fate of the poor climbing boys—children who can barely walk forced into frighteningly dark, not to mention, dangerous chimneys by older boys with lighted tapers. Their death rate is appalling, their treatment worse."

"Enough. I get the picture." The earl halted her on-slaught. "You're quite well-spoken for a country chit, not to mention well versed on the issues."

"Papa believed even females should be educated to their fullest capabilities. Something you would dun him for, I'm certain." Sarcasm fell heavily from her lips.

"He thought it was a shame I was born a girl, because he knew females were not encouraged to use their intel-ligence. Said he'd like to see me at Oxford. Not that he had a great deal of respect for the college. Papa said the professors were often lazy and the students apathetic. Still and all, he would have liked to see me continue my education." She sighed. "But he's gone."

"So you're quite the bluestocking." He rolled his eyes. "This could prove *most* interesting."

"If I agree to come with you."

His lips tightened. "You have no choice in the mat-ter, Miss Angella Denning."

Eyes flashing, Angella jerked suddenly, causing the kitten to meow in protest. Quickly soothing the animal, Angella said, "Only if you have a job for me. I will not sit in your pocket."

"Stuff and nonsense, you're the most irritating, im-pertinent, difficult female it has been my misfortune to know in an age." An image of Margaret flashed in his mind. "Almost, anyway." He quickly wiped away the image of the woman determined to become his wife. It wasn't something he liked to think about.

Angella actually grinned at his condemnation as though he'd complimented her. "Thank you, m'lord. You do me honor. Now, about that job?"

"We'll see." The earl found himself grinning back at her. Her independence was a refreshing trait after Margaret's cloying dependence on his person—and his purse. "For now, I want you to be my guest." He raised a restraining hand. "Now, don't fly up in the boughs. Not now, at any rate. All right."

Since there was no gainsaying him, Angella turned away. The flush on her pale cheeks told the earl she was ashamed at her outburst, but not enough to give him the satisfaction of an abject apology. He grinned. At least she was no whimpering female given to a fit of the vapors at the first sign of inconvenience.

If she spoke the truth of the matter, she had outfaced the new vicar before the gathering of the whole village. She must have had some idea of the outcome. Glancing her way, he gazed into the large eyes of the cat lying in her lap, regarding him intently. He chuckled as he urged on his horses. Mayhap his visit would not be quite as dull as he had imagined. He wasn't sure whether he liked the idea or not.

Silence reigned as they sped on through another village and down a long road. As the sun drew behind the growing bank of clouds, Angella shivered in her lightweight gown. "Here, let me give you my jacket."

"No, thank you. I'll be fine." Angella hugged her arms to her chest.

The earl's lips tightened almost imperceptibly, but, though he did not press the issue, he did hasten the pace. Sometime later after he turned off the main road, the earl commented. "Ever been to Lucashire Hall?"

Angella nodded.

"Oh, yes," he said, "my birthday celebration."

She added, "And my brother, Edward's, commissioning reception."

"Then you know," said the earl, "we're coming on it presently."

He tooled the horses over a bridge that spanned a wide shallow stream, meandering off into the distance. "Used to be part of the moat when Lucashire Hall was Lucashire Castle."

He caught her interest. "What happened?"

The earl grinned more to himself than at her. Bluestocking indeed. The chit thirsted for knowledge, and, where Lucashire was concerned, he was more than willing to accommodate her.

"Unfortunately it was breached, raided and destroyed when one of my illustrious ancestors found himself out of grace with good King Henry III. His son, Edward, was more understanding of the circumstances and restored both our lands and titles. Been passed on ever since."

Coming down the long drive, the earl pulled the phaeton to a halt. Sweeping his arm before him, he exclaimed, not without considerable pride, "There it is, Lucashire Hall. I never tire of this view."

The huge edifice never failed to impress him whenever he came home. This was his home. The look of wonder on the face of the young woman beside him satisfied some need within him. No doubt she felt about his home as he did himself. Clasping his arm, Angella sucked in a deep breath.

"It's like something out of a dream, isn't it?" She whispered as though speaking aloud would make it disappear into the mist that surrounded it in the afternoon that had turned to damp chill.

He watched her take in the imposing residence with its main four-story facade flanked by two high round towers with their sculptured stone balustrades. The center portion of the hall was domed and a wide entrance flayed out in two long shallow-stepped staircases around a marble fountain set in a small, immaculate flower garden, ablaze with color.

Water spouted high in the air from the sculpted figure of a draped cupid poised with an arrow in his bow. On either side of the hall, well-manicured formal lawns and gardens spread out in concentric circles.

The whole of it took away her powers of speech. Taking in the beauty, Angella was scarcely aware when they arrived. The earl gave over the reins and came to lift her down. She gasped and automatically held on to the awakened kitten and her satchel as the earl's large hands spanned her tiny waist.

A moment later, her arm tucked in his, she found herself ascending the elegant stairs. The kitten dug its claws into her shoulder and huddled close to Angella's neck as she looked around the place she had visited only twice.

A giggle escaped Angella's lips.

"What is it, little Angella," the earl asked. She liked the way her name rolled off his tongue. The warmth with which he spoke her name brought a flush to her cheeks.

"I feel like Cinderella coming to the ball, sans elegant gown and glass slippers." Her giggle stilled in a choked sob.

Tightening his grip on her arm, the earl led her through the massive door, opened by an imposing butler, into the spacious vestibule with its mosaic flooring, two-story-high intricately carved ceiling and its tapestried walls. The chamber seemed to go on endlessly in either direction. Angella stared.

Giving over his cape and hat to the austere butler, the earl indicated the room. "This was once the great hall of the castle. 'Twas the only part left partially standing after the razing. The whole of the new hall was built around it. Impressive, is it not?"

Angella nodded. "It makes me feel so, so insignificant. Who am I to be in such a grand place? You are right to be proud of calling this your ancestral home."

"Glad you approve." The earl smiled. "Come. Let me show you around." He acted like a small boy showing off a prize. That picture made him more accessible, more human.

He stopped. "Wait a minute!" Taking the kitten from Angella's arms, he handed it to the disapproving butler. "Come now, Benson, 'tis but a little cat. Have her taken out into the kitchen. Cook can feed and see to the animal. Let the staff understand this is a pet." He watched the staid butler gingerly hand the squirming animal over to a maid, who cooed over the kitten as she hastened to carry out the earl's instructions.

He also handed over her satchel to a waiting maid and instructed a room to be made ready for Angella.

With a mischievous grin, the earl once more possessed himself of Angella's arm. He steered her into the formal dining hall with its coffered paneled ceiling. Over the massive fireplace at the far end was the earl's coat of arms. Danish marble medallions hung on the opposite wall. Statuary poised in carved niches on the walls, along with a series of mirrors reflecting the long polished refectory table and the solid leather-backed chairs.

Several side tables with silver urns and dishes reposed along the walls as though waiting to be used. Like the great hall, it had a unique medieval feel.

Angella shook her head. "I can almost believe that at any moment armor-clad knights and beautifully gowned ladies will burst through these huge doors." She ran her fingers lightly over the door panels with plaques depicting the story of the prophet Daniel.

The morning hall brought them into the present with the comfortable simple lines of Sheraton. The mantel was of an elaborate French design. The ceiling a confection of lace, like the intricacy of a snowflake, a design repeated in the blue of the rug that seemed but a deeper reflection of the ceiling. Large windows and French doors opened invitingly on to the gardens.

A formal drawing room was done in antique red brocade, lit at intervals by carved figures holding aloft torches. The doorway, as well as the furniture, was gilded.

For all the lavish splendor of the other rooms of the hall, it was the library that appeared to impress Angella the most, or at least the books. The earl watched her eyes widen even farther, if possible, and heard her intake of breath as she gazed on shelf upon shelf of handsomely bound volumes in the carved and molded cabinets along the paneled walls. She did not look at the wooden ceiling imported at great cost from a fifteenth-century Italian palace or the exquisite French furniture. She barely glanced at the priceless collection of urns, vases and Egyptian and Chinese pottery lining shelves high on the walls above the cabinets.

A sigh of pure pleasure passed her lips as she moved slowly over to an open cabinet. Like someone walking in a dream, she reached out to stroke the binding of a solitary book. She opened the book reverently, touching the pages as though they were a treasure she had no right to handle. Tears glistened in her eyes as she looked up at the earl. "How wonderful it must be to have so many books at your disposal."

Moved, the earl smiled at her. "You may read any book in my library or place an order with my curator for more."

"It can't be." Replacing the book, she dashed the tears from her cheeks. "I...I told you..."

"Shh." The earl put a finger to her lips. "No argument now. I shall decide in due time what I am to do with you, but for now can you not simply accept my hospitality in the spirit in which it is given? I assure you, it is not lightly given."

She shuddered, perhaps remembering the lecherous vicar. The expression on her face spoke volumes. "Why. Why would you want to keep me here?"

The earl heard the undertone of panic. Taking her arm, he forced her to face him. Anger flashed in his eyes. "How dare you think of me in the same terms as that odious hypocrite!"

Angella stepped back, seemingly stunned not only by his towering rage, but by the ease with which he read her thoughts. "I know your reputation with the ladies. Don't you think every silly maid in the village has repeated your exploits?"

"I see. If I have such experience with women, tell me

please why I would choose to ravish a skin-and-bones nobody like you?" His eyes narrowed. "Besides, what would you do if I did? You are without proper chaperone here in my domain, and I shall not have some half-witted annoying female relative live in just to provide you with such."

He took a deep breath before continuing.

"The servants would not raise a finger to help you whatever I chose to do. Fact is, you have nowhere to go, no one else to whom to turn. Now, get off your high horse and comport yourself like the gently bred female you purport to be."

"Purport to be!" Angella faced him down, eyes blazing. "You pompous aristocrat. You are just like my arrogant grandfather. I did not bespeak your help, and I'll do well enough without it. Now, I'll collect my cat and be on my way. M'lord!" She made for the door.

With a grunt of irritation, the earl hauled her back. "How dare you spurn my generosity? Right now, in the absence of your brother, it appears I'm your guardian. I'll not have you traipsing off somewhere."

Angella stamped her foot in frustration. "I will not stay where my honesty is called into question." She blinked back tears. "Isn't it enough the 'good' people of Cambrage overset everything my father taught about love and forgiveness and acceptance? I expect to be treated with respect."

"Stop acting like a spoiled child, then."

"I am not!" Even as her voice rose, Angella cringed. "Well…"

She let out a surprised squeak when the earl lightly picked her up and carried her up the wide staircase with its gilded banister to a well-appointed bedchamber. There, to the obvious surprise of the housekeeper who was readying the room for her, he dumped her on the bed.

"Mrs. Karry, see that Miss Denning receives a proper bath. Let her sleep awhile, then find her a decent gown. I wish her to join me for dinner." He grinned at Angella's repressed outrage as he spoke to the matronly housekeeper.

"By the by, Mrs. Karry, lock the door when you leave her. Not that she'd get far with that banged-up knee of hers."

He gave one last glance at Angella's face before he turned to go. Whether it was red with embarrassment or anger he knew not, but he suspected the latter.

Chapter 3

Angella cringed with embarrassment. "I…I'm sorry to be such a bother."

The matronly housekeeper surveyed the young woman with some surprise. "You aren't what I expected," she managed to say.

Angella got the impression the housekeeper expected a haughty sophisticate or a bedecked cyprian.

Angella seemed to bring out the woman's protective motherly instincts. "You'll be fine, miss. I've raised eight children of my own. Jest don't figure why the earl took you under his wing." She shut her lips to keep from saying anything further and glanced around the room. "At least the maids did the room up right."

Angella, her arms hugging her chest, shivered in the chill of the room. The fire in the hearth, though lit, had not had time to warm the room and sent more noise than heat or light into the large well-appointed chamber.

She doubted much of anything missed the eagle eyes of the motherly housekeeper. She also doubted the space needed more than clean sheets to make it presentable. The mahogany dresser glowed with its recent polish, the gilt mirror above it reflected the highly polished escritoire with its three shelves of books, as well as the dark wood armoire across the room.

The books drew Angella's interest. If she were not so cold, she would have limped over to examine the titles. As it was, she shook as if with fever. Her knee ached. She closed her eyes, willing herself to be still, but to no avail.

The housekeeper noticed, and rushed to throw a blanket around her. Angella smiled tremulously. "Th-thank you."

Her gaze assessing, Mrs. Karry drew the blanket more tightly around her. "Denning. Hmm. You related to Reverend Denning? A good man that. Too bad he passed on."

Tears glistened in Angella's eyes as she nodded. "My father."

Angella read sympathy in her expression when she spoke. "Have no relatives ta take you in, I take it? Shame that. I suppose the good people of Little Cambrage refused to help. Well, never you mind about that. The earl expects loyalty and obedience, but he is fair…he is. Like his father. Not many know that he has not been off in London with no care for us here." She chatted familiarly, making Angella feel more comfortable as the woman directed the maids in preparing the bath on the rug by the fire.

"I knows how often the manager goes in to London ta ask the earl's advice. Often, he does. And that secretary of his is here leastways twice a month. Time the earl came home, though. Been gallivanting off in London far too long." She continued talking as she hustled the slender young woman into the lilac-scented water.

"He—he…di-didn't…ch-choose…the…n-new… v-vicar," stuttered Angella, allowing the garrulous housekeeper to assist her out of her gown and into the scented bath.

Sighing, she sank into the hot water, letting the heat flow over her cold skin.

It took forever for the warmth of the water to soak into her chilled body. Finally the warmth penetrated and Angella's eyes closed drowsily. It had been so long since she had taken a full bath, not, in truth, since her father fell ill.

Without assistance, she had been unable to manage either the tub or the heavy jugs alone, and her mother had been too busy nursing her father to help her. After her mother got ill, she had done little more than splash water on her hands and face, for she'd turned to nursing both her mother and father.

Several women from the village helped out when they could, leaving food and washing the soiled linens, but others, fearing contagion, stayed away. When her father succumbed first, Angella had little time to spare for tears or grief. Day and night she stayed beside the bed of her mother, nursing her, willing her to open her eyes, praying for her recovery.

Her desperate prayers went unanswered. With one last shallow breath, her mother passed on. She smiled in the end, glad to be meeting her husband on the other side. Never had Angella felt so bereft.

After her mother's death, Angella had given way

to her grief. She wept until she had no tears left, then, swallowing the gigantic lump in her throat, she got up. Wiping her face, she sat at her father's desk resolutely and took up a pen.

Dipping into the plain ink pot, she began a letter to her brother. In her neat flowing handwriting, she explained the circumstances surrounding their parents' deaths.

Dear Edward,
It is my grievous duty to inform you of the death of both Mother and Father.

As I am alone now with no idea of how to go on, I pray you will see your way clear to return home at least for a time.

I shall write Grandfather to acquaint him with the passing on of his daughter. I will tell him, also, of my need, but I sincerely doubt he will heed my letter any more than he heeded the letters Mother wrote since her marriage to Father.

Wherever I go, I will try to leave word here at the vicarage so you can find my direction and come to me directly.

I am sorry to be the one to give you this news, but as you know, there is no one else.

If you're wondering about Mrs. Adams, who so faithfully looked after us since we were children in leading strings, she passed on some six months past.

Please come home, Edward.
Ever your sister,
Angella

As she wrote, tears started again and dotted the stiff parchment. Folding it, she addressed it and sent it off posthaste. Her prayers went with that letter, along with her doubts.

Would Edward receive the letter? Would he return? Even if he did, it would be months before she could expect him. What would happen to her in the meantime?

The next task was more difficult. Reluctantly she sat and wrote to her grandfather. The returned, unopened missive taunted her.

While she waited for word from Edward, she spent time with the one woman in the village who truly cared for her mother and did what she could for Angella. Unfortunately, she was infirm and not well situated herself and Angella refused to be a further drain on the elderly woman's resources. The emotional support she received made up for what the dear woman was unable to supply materially.

Angella thought back to when Reverend Carter arrived to take over the living. Could things have turned out differently? She didn't see how they could have. Seeing a young woman in the vicarage he thought to be empty and ready for his occupancy, he looked her over. The young lad at his side grinned at her. Reverend Carter asked, "Who are you?"

When she explained, he ran a finger over his lips as he assessed her person until she shifted, uncomfortable under his close scrutiny.

"I…I had no place to go and did not know how long it would be before someone would be appointed to the living." Angella paused. Something about the vicar made her uneasy, yet she had nothing on which to base her feelings. "I thought I'd hear from my brother or grandfather before you arrived." She paused and waited for Reverend Carter to speak.

He narrowed his gaze. "Are there bedchambers enough?"

"Yes, three. As well as living quarters for the house-keeper. She lives in."

"I see." Angella and the vicar's son followed as the large man walked through the small vicarage. Angella tried to point out how well her parents kept things up. She showed him her father's study, which had always been inviting and filled with books. The vicar merely grunted.

"It will do for now. Temporary living at best." He asked other questions Angella tried to answer to the best of her knowledge, but her heart sank. This wasn't the sort of man she hoped to take her father's place. He didn't seem to care when she spoke about the congregation, he made derogatory comments about the vicarage and snapped at his son for little or no reason.

Angella wasn't even certain what to do. Yet at the end of the tour as they returned to the front room, Reverend Carter said, "I take it no one has offered to take you in?"

Angella glanced at her worn shoes and up again. "No. Though, if someone would assist me, I'd go to Lucashire Hall." She paused. "Mother suggested that I appeal to the Earl of Lucashire."

"I see." A small smile tugged at the corners of the man's mouth. It was not the nicest of smiles, but Angella thought she was being overly sensitive in the situation. After all, she'd lived in the house for the past ten years—happy years. She gulped back a sob. If the vicar turned her out, where would she stay the night and beyond?

After a long, scary interval, the vicar nodded as though to himself. "Good. Very good. It should work out." He all but muttered to himself. With a nod, he addressed Angella. "My dear, it behooves me as the keeping of the ministry to provide for my fellow vicar's child. I shall allow you to live here with my son and me for the time being. We'll see what the future holds." His gaze narrowed as he waited for her reply.

Despite her reservations, Angella breathed a sigh of relief when he invited her to stay on. Her relief did not last. The past few weeks went through her mind, stopping with her timely rescue by the earl. Was this God's intervention or another horror to endure? She closed her eyes and sighed.

Now as she sat in the bath, she relished the housekeeper's hands washing her hair. The long tresses, heavy with water, felt clean for the first time in ever so long.

"Miss Angella, we must get you out or you'll get chilled again. The water is right cold." Chiding the girl as if she was a child, Mrs. Karry helped her from the bath and toweled her dry. As she pulled a warm nightgown over her head, Angella exclaimed, "Where did this come from?"

The housekeeper sat her down by the dresser to dry, comb and braid her hair. "'Tis left over from when His Lordship's sisters were young."

Angella smoothed down the soft material. It had been a long time since she had worn something so fine. "How many sisters?"

"Three. All married and scattered."

She yawned. Not long thereafter, Mrs. Karry tucked her into the large bed under the thick green coverlet.

"There now. Sleep tight. I'll be waking you in time for dinner."

"Thank you…Mrs. Karry." Angella's eyes closed and she slept even before the housekeeper left the room.

In the sitting room next to his bedchamber, the earl stared out at the darkening sky. Beneath the tall windows, flower and herb gardens, pleasure lawns and parks stretched away to the far wood where he had played as a child. Beyond them was the oblong lake where he and his sisters spent so many happy hours when he was but a lad in leading strings.

He had been quite the pest, but his sisters, who were older, put up with him with good grace. It had been a long time since he had seen Ellen. She seemed happy, if sometimes rather lonely, with her baron and three children in Lancashire. Many a time she invited him to visit, but he never found the time. He wished now he'd gone, if only to get to know his nieces and nephew.

As for Doris, he hadn't seen her since the laird took her away to live with him in his castle in the Scottish highlands. From her scarce letters, he knew she had one son and longed for more. This he learned from Darlene, his youngest sister, whose eyes still flashed with laughter whenever he saw her. She once assisted him in his shenanigans. She, too, was married and had… Was it three or four little ones? Always one more in the basket. She always did love little ones. He thought, now, he should have spent more time with her, too.

He well knew why he stayed away. Being closer to him in both age and temperament, she was not above scolding him for neglecting his responsibilities. He justified himself quickly. It was not as though he did

not take care of his family. As of last count his purse
stretched to three aunts, two great uncles, and a host
of cousins and other distant relatives. He knew at least
four relatives in the ministry owed their living to him.

The thought brought a frown to his lips. Why hadn't
the living at Little Cambrage been offered to one of his
blood? He should have looked into the situation at the
time. Dimly, he recalled his man of business asking
him about it. Somehow, the thought hadn't penetrated
that Reverend Denning had died and not moved on to
a more lucrative situation.

His hands fisted at his sides at the thought of Angella's plight. Had he been taking his responsibilities
seriously, he would have known about her and about the
new vicar. That is, if she'd told the truth, and he was
more than half convinced she had.

A cynical smile touched his lips. He deserved her
condemnation and he deserved to be saddled with an
unfledged chit. Letting his mind wander, he dressed
her in the finest of satins and silks. His hands itched
to caress that thick hair. He could well afford to provide for her.

Thankfully, his father's wise investments meant that
when the war was over and farm prices went bust, his
pockets would remain deep. The earl hoped his own investments proved as fruitful. He kept his farms in good
repair, his tenants content.

Unlike some of his acquaintances, who lived far beyond their means or lost their money in bad investments
and had to sell off their country estates, his own estate
was secure. His lips twisted cynically. He knew many
of his beggared peers continued to comport themselves
about London as though their pockets were not to let.

As head of the family, he took care not to squander his money unwisely. This time his cynicism turned inward as he recalled the gowns, jewels and fripperies with which he had delighted his flirts. At least he had left none of his family destitute—not if he knew their plight. This even extended to a profligate nephew of Ellen's. He smiled as he thought about his aunt Helga and favorite young cousin, Betsy. He'd rescued his cousin out of awkward social situations more than once. His thoughts turned to Angella, who was of an age with Betsy. How could a grandfather so cut off his own flesh and blood, that his granddaughter had not even a roof over her head?

Angrily the earl turned from the window. He stopped beside the large kidney-shaped desk behind which his father used to sit as he worked. He used to think his father too straitlaced, always concerned with his estate.

Now-remembered incidents gave the earl fresh insight. His father had cared—truly cared—not only about the estate, but also about each servant, each farmer and worker in his employ. It was because of this concern he had not wanted his son squandering his life needlessly in the war. The earl had never seen things in this light before. He still wasn't sure he agreed, but at least he understood.

Angella, too, was now under his care, though by default. Striding to the wall, the earl tugged at the gold-tasseled bellpull.

A liveried footman answered the summons. "M'lord?"

"Tell Trowbridge I wish to see him." He paced the room as he awaited the secretary. He had done well snapping up the ex-soldier as soon as he arrived in London looking for work. He had found the short, solid man both loyal and enterprising.

Brushing a shock of blond hair from his eyes, the secretary entered the room. "M'lord, if it's about the invitations, I have almost finished writing your regrets. I also saw to flowers for Lady Margaret before leaving London this forenoon."

The earl interrupted him. "You knew I brought a young woman back with me."

A slow flush crept up the secretary's cheeks. "Yes, m'lord, I was aware of this."

Not for the first time the earl wondered how a man as naive as Trowbridge managed the rough, often raucous life of a soldier. He knew him to be a man of action who chafed under the restraints of desk and chair.

"Miss Angella is in immediate need of a complete wardrobe from the inside out. I would have you go to London to get her fitted out in all that is fashionable. You well know, since of course you handle the bills brought me, which modistes on Bond Street with whom I prefer to deal.

"The girl needs footwear, as well, so see to her foot size when you get her other measurements from Mrs. Karry. Oh, and, Trowbridge. She needs them straightaway, so be sure to bring as much as possible back with you on the morrow. Have the rest delivered to my house in London and see that they're sent on."

Pacing the floor, he clasped his hands behind his back. Glancing up, he witnessed the speculation in the eyes of the secretary. "You'll enjoy the trip. Yes, and let the modiste know I am not above offering incentives for work completed speedily and well."

"Ahem. Do you wish me to bring back a bauble or two for the…lady?" The implication made the earl frown.

"Miss Angella Denning is the orphaned daughter of the former vicar of Little Cambrage, not some light-skirt, Trowbridge."

The secretary flushed. "My apologies, m'lord. I had no notion."

Stilling the man's stuttered apology with a raised hand, the earl commanded. "Enough. 'Tis enough you know it now. Please acquaint the staff with the situation."

"I'll leave tonight, m'lord." Trowbridge leaned forward eagerly.

"And give the highwaymen or the footpads an opportunity to waylay you? I don't think so. First light is soon enough." He clapped a hand on the smaller man's shoulders. "Besides, I have another mission for you to do for me this day yet. About Miss Denning…" He explained tersely, well knowing this was the sort of task the former soldier relished.

"I'll leave straightaway. I wouldn't think it would take long to find the truth of the matter."

"Good. As soon as you return, let me know what you discover, but for the moment I'd as soon no one knew where the girl is. No need to submit her to any more village tittle-tattle than necessary." He laughed at his presumption. "Of course, we tooled directly through the village, so I imagine the village tabbies are already spreading falsehoods. You may have to dig for the truth, Trowbridge."

"I quite understand, m'lord." With a precise about-face, Trowbridge hastily exited the room. As the door closed, the earl's gaze narrowed in thought. Soon he'd know the truth about the young woman under his roof. Was she an opportunist seeking his favor or, in truth, the destitute daughter of the vicar? Did it matter?

In good conscience he could not throw her out, though mayhap he could offer a job as she was so insistent—if she was who she claimed, that is. He thought of her seeming innocence, her intelligence, her sensitivity.

A London season? No, he turned violently from the thought. He'd not have the chit's head turned by all the false glitter. But, of course, she was in mourning and that was excuse enough to keep her out of circulation for the time being.

The girl needed a companion. Against all convention, he shied from adding to his household. He returned to Lucashire for peace and quiet and had no intention of disturbing it further. The girl was here on his leave. She'd abide by his mandates or find herself another protector.

Another protector? Why did he feel so strongly he must protect her? Most like he needed protection from her scathing judgment. The chit was too quick-witted by half. He growled at the thought of her harsh judgments not only of his society, but also of his lifestyle.

Even if the opinion of his peers paralleled hers, he was much too much of a gentleman to make a cake of himself by parading her out-of-fashion attitudes before the critical ton.

He could see Angella spouting her opinions in the drawing rooms of London to the dismay of the hostesses. The thought brought a faint smile to his lips. Would be interesting, that. But, no. The girl had little tact and less polish.

If his personage awed her not, he shuddered to think

what she might say to a member of the royal family. Would she go so far as to ring a peal over the head of the Duke of York? One of his mistresses sold military commissions. It led to his stepping down from his post for a time. No, better keep the chit under wraps here at the hall.

He chuckled to himself. Did she truly expect to be put to work? He'd seen her dainty hands. They weren't used to physical labor. Probably some fustian to engender his sympathies. Then again, if she wanted gainful employment… Baser thoughts sparked his eyes.

Thoughts of her genuine fright when she talked about the vicar quelled his speculations in that direction. Not that he'd force her into an untenable position. He'd not do something as sordid as that. He frowned. Then, what made his idea any less reprehensible than what the vicar sought? At least the man offered marriage.

His own reawakened conscience smote him. Stuff and nonsense. His mother would be disappointed in his thoughts and his present lifestyle. His gentle mother taught him so differently. He bowed his head. No. He hadn't returned to Lucashire to be reminded of his lady mother, though he sensed she would have liked the feisty young woman he'd brought with him.

Striding toward the window, he stared out over his vast estate. The lawns stretched toward the parklands, grass, trees and hedges perfectly trimmed and kept. How different from his life.

He thought to escape the feeling of being out of control by leaving London. Angella herself left him feeling even more helpless. He wondered if she'd like the clothes he ordered. What nonsense! Of course she would. He needed to take care not to turn her head or he'd have another rapacious woman hanging out his pocket.

One woman was not so different from another after all. Mayhap he should have Trowbridge bring back as he put it, "A bauble or two." That would add sparkle to the chit's eyes. A ruby—no, emeralds—to set off her wondrous green eyes.

Depending on whether or not his secretary's findings confirmed her story, he'd let her stay—on his terms. Actually he rather liked the idea of crossing swords with the chit. A smile of anticipation crossed his face as he sauntered into his bedchamber to dress for dinner.

Chapter 4

That first night, they declared war over the silliest of things—wine. The core problem was her deep-seated sense of right and wrong.

As the liveried servant leaned over to fill her goblet, Angella smiled sweetly and covered it with her hand. "Thank you, no."

The servant glanced toward the earl for direction. He looked at Angella. "May I ask what is the problem?"

"There is no problem," said Angella in some surprise. "'Tis simply that, as a Christian, I do not indulge in alcoholic beverages of any kind."

"It's not as though you are going to become bosky over one glass of wine with dinner. It is expected. Are you saying someone cannot be a Christian and have a bit of wine now and again?" Actually the earl wasn't certain why her action irritated him so much.

Her lips turned up. "Of course not. Though, I believe

it best in this age of drunkenness and overindulgence to set a good example for others. I simply choose not to befuddle my thinking in any manner or do anything which might shame my Lord."

"Is that what you're accusing me of doing?" The earl half rose, his own guilt adding to his fury. "This is ridiculous. I expect you to act like a lady and accept my generosity."

Angella's eyes narrowed in a way he was beginning to recognize as the first sign of trouble. "How kind of you, I'm sure," she said with exaggerated politeness. "However, I believe I was quite polite in my refusal, so why make an issue of it? I doubt you'd kick up such a fuss with any other guest in your house."

"Other guests are invited."

Angella paled. "I don't drink and that's that." Her chin lifted defiantly.

"I say wine is part of dinner and, as long as you reside under my roof, I expect you to humor my wishes." His smile was meant to defuse the situation. "You've lived in the country all your life, I realize. As quick-witted as you appear to be, there is no reason you cannot learn the basics expected of those in polite society."

"I beg to differ, m'lord. You insult my lady mother. Even you must acknowledge she would know what to teach me."

"How well did you learn the lessons?" muttered the earl.

Lifting her head with a dignity that elicited the earl's admiration, Angella said, "Now you insult me, m'lord. Your own manners are to let."

For a long moment they glared at each other. The earl dropped his gaze first. Botheration, the chit bearded him in his own household. The last thing he needed was some unfledged chit pointing out his faults. Why did her presence make him feel so guilty?

Through narrowed eyes, Angella stared at him. Gracefully she lay down her napkin and pushed herself to her feet. She grimaced as though in pain, but she obviously ignored any discomfort.

Once standing, she continued to be deadly polite. "Then, m'lord, you will excuse me if I no longer accept your hospitality." She marched toward the startled footman, hesitating at the door.

"Go on and pout in your room if you wish, but don't expect dinner to be brought up to you. I don't pander to childishness." He heard the door close after her. The footman kept his expression neutral, but the earl sensed his disapproval. What did he care about the servants? That was a lie and he knew it.

Nevertheless, the earl continued eating, ignoring the silence Angella left in her wake. It irritated him that he felt very alone without the prickly presence of the pastor's daughter.

Some minutes later Mrs. Karry hesitantly entered the room. Agitated, she fingered the jangling keys at her side. "M'lord, might I have a word?"

"What is it?" He was not used to having his dinner interrupted and it quite overset his digestion, not to mention his enjoyment. With a sigh, he set aside his thick prime cut of beef, which he usually ate with such relish.

"'Tis Miss Angella, m'lord. She be leaving."

"What is she doing? Having you pack for her?" The housekeeper had told him about providing the girl with a few of his sister's things she'd found in a trunk in one of the attics.

"No, m'lord. She insists on putting on her own things." She wiped a tear from the corner of her eye. "The wee thing thanked me ever so nice. Then jest walked out the door." The earl hated seeing how Angella's stubbornness about broke the faithful retainer's heart.

His patience snapped. "Well, if that's what she wants, then let her go."

Teach her a lesson, he thought. She'd be back straightaway when she realized how cold and dark and scary it was outside.

Mrs. Karry gasped. "But, m'lord, it is cold and dark. Think it may even be raining some." The good woman shuddered and the earl wondered at her depth of concern for the chit on such short acquaintance. "What if she is accosted by some dreadful highwayman?"

A laconic smile touched his lips. "Precisely, madam." He glanced at the gold chased watch hanging from his gray vest. "How long do you think she will last out there before she swallows her accursed pride and returns?"

The housekeeper eyed him with some trepidation. "I fear, m'lord, you will find she is of a rather determined stamp." Pursing her lips, she added under her breath, "Like someone else I might mention."

She left him feeling vaguely uneasy over his actions. "I vow," he grumbled, "if she is to live under my protection, she's going to have to accept my authority." After eating a bite or two more, he shoved away his plate and motioned for the flunky waiting for his summons. His appetite fled and he demanded his port.

Though usually abstemious, he deliberately spent

much time slowly sipping his drink, expecting that any moment someone would inform him the girl had returned, wet mayhap, but cowed and submissive. He waited in vain.

Finally in a fit of temper, he left the dining room for the library. The book room brought back the look of awe on Angella's face when he showed it to her and the radiant light in her eyes when he offered to let her read any book of her choice.

Out of countenance as much with himself as with Angella, he hunkered down in a wingback chair before the roaring hearth. "She'll be back," he told himself, but his protestations became weaker, his guilt heavier and his concern greater as the clock ticktocked away the minutes.

After leaving the grand dining hall, Angella made her way to her room, her head high. Tears threatened to fall, but she forced them back. Phooey on the man anyway. He had no right to force her to do something she did not think right—none at all. She hadn't been obnoxious about it. He was as high-handed in his own way as the vicar.

Obviously this was not going to work out. "Well, Lord, it's just You and me again."

Mrs. Karry had found her throwing on her old clothes and pulling on her tattered shoes. At Mrs. Karry's cry, she'd tersely explained. "I cannot stay in a place where my values are not respected."

After trying to persuade the girl to stay, Mrs. Karry threw up her hands. Rummaging in the closet, she came back with a worn gray wool cape. Mrs. Karry insisted she at least take the old cape. "'Tis no good to anyone else. You might as well take it."

Eyeing the worn cape, Angella thought how nice it would feel against the cold. "You sure no one would mind? I won't be taking what isn't mine."

"Please, let me do this for you. It is a gift."

"Thank you, Mrs. Karry, you are the kindest person I have met since my parents died. If you will, pray for me."

After giving the dismayed housekeeper a warm hug, Angella slipped down to the kitchen. There, Angella took up the kitten she found snuggling in a box fixed up by the cook.

"She's a bit of a thing," said the robust woman, gently petting the kitten on the head. "Taking her with you, are you? 'Tis nasty out there."

When Angella hesitated, the cook added, "She is safe here with me. Be a good mouser by-and-by."

"You're right," Angella said as she forced a smile. Cuddling the animal close a moment, she carefully set her back in her box. "Goodbye," she whispered.

"I'll leave her in your care then. Thank you." With a single backward look, she left the fairy-tale world behind. 'Twas but a dream after all.

At the bridge, she turned again. Rain had begun to fall and she pulled the cape more closely about her shoulders. Though old, it was thick, but not thick enough to keep out the biting cold that inched in from every opening. Hunching her shoulders, she walked down the road, trusting the Lord to keep her safe.

The moon peeped out now and again from behind the clouds as the rain continued to fall. Before long, Angella shivered with cold. She tried not to think about a future without the overwhelming earl. Phooey, what nonsense! The man was the most odious personage, other than the vicar, she had ever met. "I guess men are very much alike," she muttered.

She was distracted by her thoughts, and 'twas by instinct only she moved to the side of the road to avoid being run over by a gig coming down the road at a fast clip. Pulling her cape more closely about her shoulders, she turned away from the driver.

"Foolish woman," complained the driver, seeing her walking alone along the roadside.

Angella stumbled along until she all but fell to her knees in exhaustion. The warmth and light of the distant hall tantalized her. Her aching body begged her to return. Her set-to with the earl seemed as foolish as her temper.

For a moment she stood, then turned around. Even took a step. Her thin shoes splashed water onto the already damp hem of her gown. Tears mingled with the rain pouring down her cheeks. "He was wrong!" she declared to no one in particular.

A clap of thunder drowned out her cry. The thunder cut her like heavenly judgment. Her temper again. Would she ever learn to control it? Still and all, she could not return to a man who would force her to do things she felt were wrong, could she? If she gave in this time, what would he demand of her next? At the thought, Angella straightened her shoulders and turned back to the road, away from Lucashire Hall.

Not that it mattered. Her feet slipped and she fell into the mud. With effort, she managed to leverage herself upright. She must find shelter, and quickly. Edging carefully off the road, she stumbled into a stand of trees. Slumping against a trunk, she slid to the wet ground.

Cold and miserable, she tried to pray, but her mind felt as frozen as her limbs. Shaking, she ducked her head as rain dripped down on her through the branches. Even the cold and her shivering frame could not keep her awake.

As she drifted off, she thought wearily, *Mayhap I'll not wake up. Where are You, Lord?* Would He take her home to be with Mama and Papa? A weak smile spread on her blue lips as she thought of their bright faces and heard their laughter.

In the library, Benson announced the secretary. Trowbridge strode into the room, a smile of satisfaction on his lips. "I got the information you requested."

The earl eyed him wearily. Carefully he sat the cold cup of coffee on the table next to him. His unease had grown steadily as time passed and the girl did not return. Still, he was unwilling to admit defeat. "What have you found?" He stood facing away from the hearth. The heat seared his back.

Standing beside the earl, Trowbridge spread out his hands to the fire. "Seems the girl is Reverend Denning's daughter. She had indeed made inquiries about you, without much success. No one seemed too eager to be of assistance to me, and, I gathered, to her, either."

"That new vicar?"

Trowbridge rolled his eyes. "A more sanctimonious pompous man you've yet to find. He had a good bit to say about the girl." He shook his head. "To hear him tell it, the girl was out for the main chance."

"He said he was trying to be kind to the girl, but

that wasn't enough for her." Trowbridge grinned. "He sent a warning to you, Lordship. He claims Miss Denning is a, in his words, a scheming hussy." Trowbridge cleared his throat as the earl frowned. "His words, not mine, m'lord.

"He also mentioned she was wanton and that cat of hers was pure evil."

The earl studied the man, facing him. He'd learned to trust Trowbridge's instincts. "What do you think?"

Trowbridge hesitated. "He made a good case against Miss Denning, but I had the distinct feeling he was selling me a bill of goods. As I left the vicarage, his young son pulled me aside. Making certain his father did not see us, he gave me another story entirely. I could tell he was scared to death of his father, but he must have been listening to the vicar's accusations."

The earl leaned forward slightly. "What did the boy have to say?"

"He asked me if the nice lady was safe. He told me she had always been kind to him. He said, as much as he would have liked her to be his mother, he was glad she was gone."

Trowbridge pursed his lips. "The lad told me 'I was afraid Father would hurt her as he did my mother.' He did not say in so many words, m'lord, but I got the feeling the man beat the boy. Besides, I also spoke to another old woman who had adored the girl's mother.

"She told me the whole of it was a setup and she believed not a word of what the vicar or the other villagers said about the young woman. If she had not been old and ill, she herself would have taken the girl in. Said the girl is as sweet and caring as her lady mother. I believed her."

Turning, the earl stared into the fire. It still boiled down to believing or not believing the girl herself. Stuff it all! Why didn't she return? He realized suddenly that Trowbridge had not left.

"Is there something else?"

The secretary pushed his damp hair from his eyes. "Just a bit worrying, m'lord. On the road I passed what I thought was a woman walking along the road. She was all alone. The more I think of it, the odder it seems."

The earl tensed. "You didn't recognize her?"

"'Twas raining and I was in a hurry to return. She turned away when I passed. The more I think of it, the more I think there was something furtive about her."

Striding to the door, the earl yelled for a footman. "Has Miss Angella returned?"

The butler reappeared with the answer. "No, m'lord. No one has seen her since she left."

Straightening, the earl called for a carriage. "Trowbridge, come on. I want you to show me exactly where you passed that woman."

Not long thereafter, Trowbridge sat beside the earl in a curricle as the earl hurried the black horses along the road. The earl's eyes darkened in anger and concern. Through the rain, he peered from side to side. Beside him, his secretary did the same until Trowbridge called out. "Here. This is where I saw her. At least…I'm pretty sure it was here."

Slowing, the earl tooled along that section of road. "Where is she?" growled the earl through gritted teeth.

"She might have fallen, I suppose."

Trowbridge understood only that the girl had gone of her own accord.

Other thoughts paraded through the earl's mind and

he cursed himself for not stopping the chit. "Should have locked her in her room," he grunted to himself.

To his surprise a prayer leaped to his lips. "Help me find her, Lord." It wasn't much, but certainly more than he had spoken to the Almighty in many a year.

Ahead was a stand of trees. Mayhap she sought shelter. 'Twas a good place to hide from searchers along the road. Then again, she had no reason to suspect he'd come after her. Mayhap she didn't wish to be seen by anyone heading toward the hall.

Pulling up the team, he handed the reins into the secretary's keeping. Hopping down, the earl sent up a prayer of gratitude that the rain had become a mere drizzle and the clouds parted, allowing the light of the moon to reveal his way. His second petition of the night, he thought wryly, gingerly treading through the brush— and all due to an irritating young woman. Anger vied with anxiety as the earl moved farther down the gentle slope into the shelter of the trees.

"Where is she, Lord? Where?" A third petition, he thought with a part of his cynical mind.

A shaft of moonlight beamed down. He stopped and stared as he saw her huddled against the trunk of a tree, her face lit in the light. A hasty thank-you dropped from his lips as he squatted beside her. Was it truly an answer to his prayer?

As he touched her forehead, he felt her chill through his gloves. She groaned as he gently lifted her in his arms. Fluttering softly, she snuggled closer to him for warmth as he carried her to the curricle. With a start, she awoke as he handed her up to Trowbridge.

"Let me go," she cried out in alarm.

"Move over, Trowbridge. You drive. I'll hold the

girl." Swinging Angella more firmly into his arms, he growled, "Hush up, girl. Be still."

Angella stiffened as she recognized the voice. "Leave me be."

He did not answer as he opened his heavy coat. Holding her close, he wrapped it around them both. She shivered violently against him. "Now, relax. I'm not going to hurt you. I am taking you home. We'll settle our differences later. All right?" He felt her nod against him and smiled. It felt good to hold her, even wet and soggy as she was, in his arms. Then he frowned. Botheration! What was he to do with her?

Twas two days before Mrs. Karry permitted her to be up and about. By then Trowbridge had returned from London with the first of his purchases for Miss Denning.

As the earl suspected, Angella was delighted, at least at first, with the clothes Trowbridge brought home with him. But he had not expected her hesitance at accepting anything from him she had not earned.

He learned, rather quickly, she was indeed serious about earning her way, and no amount of argument would make her wear a stitch of the new clothing until he agreed, out of pure frustration, to let her help the curator catalog the books of the library. The overworked curator told him that he found her a delight to be around, as well as an efficient worker.

With that particular crisis averted, the earl foolishly believed things would settle down, until today, that is, when the rest of her clothes arrived and he picked out the red gown for her to wear to dinner.

As he stood outside her bedchamber now, he recalled

she had won that first round, but he was determined that she would not win every one. "Come out here, Angella."

"I will *not* come out!" Angella yelled through the locked door as the earl ineffectually pounded on the door of her bedchamber.

The earl, who had been standing at the door for several minutes trying to persuade his annoying guest to open the door and join him for dinner, was rapidly coming to a boil. "Angella Denning, come out of that room this minute."

"No!"

Grinding his teeth, he clenched his fist to keep from slamming it against the door. "Get out here right now, young lady. If you don't, I'll…I'll break down the door."

Was that a stifled giggle he'd heard from the other side? "I'd like to see you try."

Stuff! Why had he made such a ridiculous threat? The heavily ornamented door would probably withstand an army. "Angella, please. Listen to me. You have to come out sooner or later."

"Later, then. Much later."

Hanging on to his self-control with some difficulty, the earl sucked in a deep breath. Any other woman would have jumped at the chance to wear fashionable gowns from Bond Street, but not Miss Denning. Of course not. Why should she behave in a normal fashion now, when she had done nothing but wrangle with him since he first picked her up? He should have left her and that ball of fur to the tender mercies of the village.

No, he backed up. No, not that. "Angella, I'll give you another minute and then I'm calling Mrs. Karry for the key."

"Do that, but I'll not come out."

"You will or…."

"Or what? You'll throw me out? Well, go right ahead. But be sure I'll change out of this piece of fluff that parades as an evening gown first. I'd rather show myself in a nightgown. It covers more." Stung by her assessment, as well as her ingratitude, the earl raised his voice. "I'll have you know that gown is in the first style of elegance."

"For whom…your latest flirt? This gown is indecent and you knew it when you picked it out for me to wear this evening."

"Come now, Angella," growled the earl, wanting to wring the girl's neck. He wasn't used to having his good taste questioned. "That gown is all the rage."

"My father would be horrified to see me in this… dreadful thing."

"Your father was a backcountry preacher."

The long pause discomfited him. He had no call to set down her father.

Was that a sob? "My father was a kind, compassionate, godly man."

"Angella, I'm sorry… I shouldn't have said that about your father. Now, will you come out?"

"Go away."

The earl clenched his teeth in frustration. His dust-ups with Angella had not ceased over the week she had resided at Lucashire. Had he thought to find peace and quiet in leaving London!

Hanging on to his rage with difficulty, he went in search of Mrs. Karry. He grabbed the key from the housekeeper's hand, then marched back to the door. After jamming the key into the lock, the earl wrenched open the door. Angry enough to throttle Angella, he strode into the room fully intending to have done with the stubborn miss under his care.

His anger died at the scene before him. Slumped on the rug in front of the hearth, Angella stared up at him through large, swollen, defeated eyes. Tears streamed down her pale cheeks.

The difference scared him. Kneeling beside her, he took her hands in his. "Angella, what's wrong? What happened? Are you all right?"

Hiccuping, she shook her head as sobs tore from deep inside. Confused, the earl drew her into his arms. "Angella. Angella, tell me what's wrong. Please?"

"Why do you want to hurt and humiliate me? Why do men want to hurt women like me? What have I done to make you think I am that kind of woman? I try to be good. Truly I do. I'm sorry if I have in some fashion, led you to believe… I mean…" She bit her lip to keep it from quivering.

"Fustian, child. What are you saying?"

Trying to control her sobs, Angella brushed her hand across her wet cheeks. "I finally understood why you wished me to wear this…this *gown.*"

He saw the horror in her face as she looked down at the now-rumpled dress. He had to admit it showed off far more than any young chit ought to show. He had not considered such when he picked it out. Most likely, many of the latest fashions from France would shock the innocent pastor's daughter.

His arms tightened around her as he felt her heart beat against his chest. "Why do you think I wanted you to wear this gown?"

"You think I am… I would…" She stared up at him,

not knowing how utterly enchanting she was with her face lovely in its very vulnerability. "I'm not… I won't."

At once the earl did understand all too clearly and he cursed himself for being so dull-witted. Guilt swept over him—for, though he had not considered making her his mistress since that first day, the thought had, at least, crossed his mind.

Looking down at Angella in her sweet innocence, he kicked himself for his arrogance. How could he ever have considered her as anything but pure and innocent or have treated her like some doxy?

"Angella, dear Angella, I think nothing of the kind. I am sorry about the gown. I did not realize it was, well, so revealing. I vow I was not attempting to seduce you, shame or hurt you in any fashion whatsoever. I have never forced myself on anyone, and I am certainly not going to begin with a young innocent under my protection."

He let her search his eyes. A tremulous smile started around her mouth. "Then I fear I rather made a cake of myself over my assumptions."

He smiled back. "We do seem to be at swords' point most of the time." Gently he pulled her to her feet. "Tell you what. I'll have Cook hold dinner while you change. Will that do?"

She smiled a radiant smile that ripped right into his cynical heart. "M'lord. Thank you."

Leaving to change out of his damp dinner jacket, the earl found himself humming as he headed toward his chamber.

Chapter 5

After their dustup about her gown, things began to change between them. From then on, he permitted her to choose her own gowns. More than one of the fashionable gowns sent out from London, were, with the able assistance of Mrs. Karry and the maid she assigned to take care of his charge, altered before Angella wore them.

He had to admit she used good taste and whatever she did to the gowns enhanced her special beauty. She looked so innocent until that mischievous twinkle sparkled out at him. Then he knew he was lost. Much easier to rail at her when she matched him rage for rage.

That happened often enough. They disagreed with each other over the latest farming techniques, which Angella insisted would increase production. He left in a towering rage—for, what could a woman know of such things? When he read up on the subject, he found her insights helpful and unusually perceptive. Apologizing had been lowering. She took it in good grace and, though she tried not to smile, he'd seen that sparkle in her eye.

They fought over the issue of slavery, though that had not been quite the same thing. The earl smiled. After a particularly delicious dinner, they sat before the roaring fire in the library, where they both felt most comfortable and in harmony with one another.

Firelight flickered over the bas-relief of the fireplace and bounced off the high ceiling. Candles dipped and rose in rhythm to the slight breeze seeping through the window and ruffling the drawn curtains.

Angella looked delectable in a high-waisted gown of forest green with a deep flounce at the hem. The sleeves puffed at the shoulder and fitted tightly to her wrists. He took note she preferred longer sleeves.

He had not even considered the topic until she pointed to drawings of the latest designs from the lady's magazine Trowbridge suggested he order for her. "Why do women parade about half-naked in the winter? Look at the short sleeves and that neckline. No wonder so many women die of pneumonia and consumption."

Startled, the earl, feeling comfortable in his waistcoat and jacket, looked down at the picture in the magazine. A young woman modeled a thin gown too scanty for the winter weather. "I never gave it a thought." An image of Margaret flashed in his mind. Always up to the mark, he now recalled her shivering in the evening's chill. He'd thought then she wanted his arms about her, and he had obliged.

The memory of the liberties taken suddenly shamed

him, and he turned from Angella's inquiring gaze. He felt sullied in the face of her innocence.

"No wonder," she continued, "so many become ill." Mischievously, she glanced up at him through her impossibly long lashes. "Of course, they do it for the likes of the gentlemen who have no notion what foolishness their women subject themselves to on their behalf."

"Um. I concede your point, Angella." He tried not to shift in the chair. Angella was much too quick and would pick up on his discomfort.

"You like women who dress like this, don't you?" Her tone was hesitant, pained.

Grimacing, the earl met her gaze. A muscle twitched in his cheek. "I agree that women dressing like that in this season are goose-witted and so are their escorts." He knew he condemned himself and his tone grew so harsh, Angella drew back.

Not one to abide hypocrisy, he hated what he was more and more seeing in himself. Stuff and nonsense. Once again, Angella found his weakness. She didn't even realize how her honesty clawed at his heart. He laughed, but there was no frivolity in the sound. "Yes, I am one of those foolish dandies. Isn't that what you wanted to know?"

Admiring Angella in her gown, the earl could not help but notice the lace that modestly covered the deep neckline. Her own addition, he supposed. A matching green ribbon held back her long tresses that glowed in the light of the fire as she settled down at his feet on a tapestried stool. He stilled his hand from reaching out to stroke the hair that glowed softly in the firelight.

As though determined to change the subject, Angella asked, "Have you ever met William Wilberforce?

Papa met him once. He was very impressed with him. Said he heard John Newton preach, too, when Reverend Newton was rector of St. Mary Woolnoth in London." She sighed. "I wish I could have heard him. To think of the influence he and Wilberforce have had in fighting the slave trade.

"Papa used to tell me how John Newton rebelled against his faith and become a shipmaster dealing in slaves. The cruelties Reverend Newton himself participated in were awful." Angella blinked. "I can't understand how anyone can be so cruel to another human being."

"Many don't think of the Africans as people, as human beings."

"So they say." Angella was indignant. "That is only an excuse. If they truly believed that, they would not deign to rape the poor women. Men don't rape animals."

"Angella," the earl told her sternly. "This is not a fit subject for a gently bred young woman."

Angella snorted. "It is that sort of attitude that allows the dreadful trade to continue."

Amused at her retort, he steered the argument. "What of Newton?"

"He became a Christian and everything changed. His whole life became not only a crusade for Christ, but also a crusade against the horrible practice of owning one's fellow human beings."

"Oh, I don't know," the earl drawled deliberately, leaning back. "Slavery is not such a bad thing after all. I've heard many slaves fare right well. They are fed and housed…"

Angella stiffened, her eyes mirroring her shock as she heard him out. He shifted uncomfortably at the disappointment on her face.

"You don't agree that the government should outlaw the slave trade, making it a criminal offense?" She paused, then swallowed. "Don't you believe, along with Wilberforce, that slavery itself must also be abolished? How is this slavery different from the serfdom from which English men—and women, I might add—fought to break out of in the Middle Ages?"

Shaking her head sadly, she murmured. "If you truly feel that way, I thank God you're not a force in the House of Lords. They're insensitive enough as it is, never seeing beyond their own comfortable livings."

The earl winced. "Now, Angella...."

"No, you listen," she said. "I suppose you'd like to return to the good old days when the lord and master of the fief had the power of life and death over his people. Sure, and why not? You wouldn't need to pay a pence to any servant on the estate." The earl could read her feelings in her expressive face. The injustice of it all tore her apart. And she was thinking worse of him by the second.

"Angella. Miss Denning," commanded the earl. "I apologize."

Gaping at him, her eyes widened. "What?"

Reaching down, he took her hand. "I was only bamming you, my dear. 'Tis ridiculously simple to set you in a spin."

As though not quite believing her ears, she continued to stare. Clearing his throat, he said, "Truth to tell, I rather admire Wilberforce. Quite the crusader. For the most part, I agree with him. Slavery is a brutal, inhuman practice that should be outlawed, totally and completely."

She really read him the riot act then, but he stopped

her with a question. "I'm curious, Angella. Why is it that you are so careful with proprieties and yet not once have you reproached me for not ordering all your gowns in black? Even a country mouse, such as you knows it's the thing to wear the willow for at least a year after the death of a close connection."

Angella stared into the hearth. "I did consider it, but not for the reason you might assume. But because I thought you might have done it deliberately. There were more important considerations at the time and, well, it just never came up. Besides, Papa never did hold with such nonsense." She smiled softly, the tendrils of her hair curling invitingly around her cheeks.

"He said, 'We who serve the Lord go on to a better place. How much better to treat others with compassion and care while they are still with us, than to pretend a great mourning when once they have gone on.' When Father and Mother died, I wore a black armband out of respect as I did not have a black gown, but I knew Papa would not want me to wear black all that long." She shrugged. "It simply was not worth wrangling about."

The earl witnessed the tears gathering in her eyes as the pain of her loss lay heavy upon her. He touched her arm lightly to comfort her. "I'm sorry about your loss, Angella. I am truly sorry."

The two sat together silently for some time. The only sound in the large chamber was the crackle of the fire, and, once in a while, the roar of the wind outside the windows. It was then the earl realized he had become rather fond of his reluctant ward.

For all their squabbles, they had much in common, from their joy in riding to their mutual desire to make the estate a model of its kind. The earl smiled at the astonishment on Angella's face when he shared his dream for Lucashire. "Fact is, I have been thinking on it for some time. You've been a help. Did you know that?" Her eyes widened.

"Me? Seems we mostly argue about how to accomplish your goals." She shivered under his tender gaze.

"True. But you forced me to do more than think about my ideas. To best you, I needed to study, and that makes me want to try that new rotation system, and…"

Angella gulped. "Oh, m'lord, I had no idea." She worried her lip. "I have been vastly unfair. I thought…"

"I care only for riotous living and my own pleasures." Though he teased, hurt flickered in his heart.

She laid a hand on his arm. "No, I knew it wasn't as bad as all that. I am sorry."

In all their brangles he'd never seen her as humble as she was at this moment. She truly cared. Looking into her eyes, he lost his train of thought.

In all the world of shallow promises and broken commitments, Angella was real. She did not play up to him for his title or his deep pockets, and she did not look down on him for not having the same deep faith as she did herself.

Yes, Miss Angella Denning was a most unusual woman, an honest woman who cared about others, cared even about his feelings. His lady mother would have liked her. Looking into her face, he wanted the peace he witnessed in her eyes, the solid faith that made her stick to her ideals no matter what. The thought startled him. He wanted more; he wanted her.

Neither could say afterward who moved first, but suddenly Angella found herself held tightly in his arms.

She melted in his gentleness, her eyes closed as though savoring the wonder of the moment.

Her heart pounded with the knowledge she had refused to acknowledge before. She was coming to care deeply for the infuriating, often odious, earl.

As he released her, she gazed up at him with all the wonder of the stars in her eyes. "M'lord...I..." She blushed, then hid her face against his broad chest.

Beneath her cheek, she felt his chest rumble in a chuckle. "Who would have thought it, little Angella? Who would have considered I would come to care about the irritating forlorn little waif I rescued from the village bullies?"

She looked up then, her eyes searching his. "You care? You truly care for me?"

His arm held her close, the tender light in his eyes reassuring her. "I can scarcely believe it myself. Truth to tell, I don't know precisely when you stopped being an irritant," he said, then paused. "Mayhap you haven't," he teased.

With a light finger, he traced her cheek. "You haven't told me what I wish to hear from you." Pulling back, he studied her face. "Am I presuming too much? This is too fast..."

When he touched her, Angella found thinking most difficult. Color stained her cheeks. "No, m'lord. I...I have come to care for you, as well." Her lashes fluttered shyly over her eyes.

He chuckled as with with deep satisfaction. Putting a finger under her chin, he forced her to look at him. "That's what I wished to hear. But, my dear Angella, this *m'lord* nonsense will not do, will not do at all. My given name is Spensor. I want to hear it from your lips."

"Spensor." She blushed. The next moment, she pushed away from him. She should not let him hold her, in any case. Whatever was she thinking? This was the Earl of Lucashire. He could have any gently bred woman to wife. Of a certain he would not choose some unfledged orphan chit from the country—not to marry.

That could mean only one thing. The pain of her thoughts brought hurt. Unable to dredge up anger, she stared at him in dismay. How could she have let this happen? How could she open her heart up to him this way? She shuddered at the ammunition she might well be handing over to him.

"What is it, Angella? What's wrong?" He tried to pull her back into his arms, but she resisted.

Tears glistened in her eyes when she turned toward him. "You've won, m'lord. I care for you, but I know not what you want of me. I am in your power, but I am not a nitwit. I know well in what category men like you place women like me who haven't the same station as yourself."

The earl flinched at her accusation. "What does a green goose like you know of the ways of the *ton*?"

Pulling away, Angella stared into the hearth, her back to him. Her head down, her shoulders bowed, she all but whispered, "I read the papers, and I hear things." She felt his anger like a physical force and felt pain deep inside.

"From the village tabbies, no doubt." He mocked her, painfully aware her accusation was not far from the man he was when he first found her by the road.

In the face of her discouragement, his own anger faded. Reaching out, he gently turned her around. "Look at me, Angella. Please."

The despondency in her eyes brought out his protective instincts. "Oh, my dear Angella, I'm no saint, but I vow I was not thinking along those lines. You are a gently bred female and I am coming to care deeply for you. I will not take liberties. That, I can promise."

The Earl of Lucashire held her gaze. "Miss Angella Denning, would you give me a chance to prove there is more to me that what you've heard?"

She searched his face, despondency giving way to hesitant shy acceptance. "I owe you that." She hesitated, then said, "But I am no match for your expertise with women. When you hold me close, it befuddles my mind. That is not good."

"I see." A laconic smile touched his lips. For the first time he realized her vulnerability without a chaperone. Mayhap, he needed to rethink that situation. Angella was an innocent. He could very easily overset her own desires by manipulating her untried feelings that had swung in his favor. He had been wrong to keep her here alone. So wrong. If for no other reason, she needed a chaperone to protect her from his newfound feelings—from his own less honorable desires.

His feelings for her as hers for him were new and precious. He must take care to hold himself to the high standards his godly mother once instilled in him—standards he put aside when he went to London. He must take care and rethink the situation.

"I've found I have much to learn from you, Angella. I admire your steadfast faith, your conviction of right and wrong—which has caused me more grief than I've known in many a day." He teased. "You have a bit of a temper."

He grinned as she flushed. "I know."

"Angella, constantly you assume the worst possible motives of me, some of which I well deserve. I need you to trust me in this, I will not treat you with disrespect." He sighed. "We've gone from swords' points to caring. I don't know beyond that, but your innocence is safe with me."

He allowed Angella to search his face. "I am coming to care for you, Spensor. I care not who you are or how deep your pockets are. But you don't know the most important person in my life."

The earl tensed. "Who are you talking about?"

"Jesus, my Savior. However we may or may not feel about each other, there can never be anything more between us unless you, too, follow Him." She stopped, hesitated. "I'm sorry. Mayhap, I am assuming too much…."

"I believed once. My mother taught me the way." He tucked a strand of hair around her ear. "I haven't exactly been living in a manner that would make my mother proud. Angella, you have something I've lost— my faith."

"It can be yours, Spensor. It's a matter of trust, trust in Jesus Christ, the Son of God who loved you so much He died on a cross to take away your sins. He took the punishment you and I deserve. He did it because of His great love. It doesn't matter what you've done. He loves you. He'll forgive. All you need do is accept what He has already done for you." Her face lit with fervor.

"You make it sound so easy. I still believe in a greater being. Isn't this enough?"

Angella shook her head. "No, you must choose to follow Him, choose to accept His gift of life."

"I see your faith means so much to you. It's why you stood up to that cravenly vicar. Why you left my home when I tried to force you to do something you felt wrong."

Angella nodded as the earl continued. "Your faith makes a difference in your life. Gives you a solid foundation and a certain peace. When," he jested, "you're not raging at me. What about people like Reverend Carter? So many Christians are nothing more than blatant hypocrites."

When Angella shuddered as she sat on the hearth rug, he said, "I'm sorry. I didn't mean to dredge up disagreeable memories."

Angella looked up at him. "What about Reverend Carter? How long will he continue at Little Cambrage?"

The earl growled. "The parishioners got what they deserved in the man after what they did to you." At her frown, he sighed. "Actually, I asked him to look for a new living and to leave once one becomes available. But I only agreed to that after he promised to send his son to live with his wife's family. The lad was anxious to go. Until then..."

"Carter stays?"

"For now, at least. Hopefully, the hypocrite won't stay long."

"Thank you for saving Andrew." Angella straightened. "But, Spensor. There cannot be a hypocrite unless there is something, someone real, and that is Jesus Christ. Besides, just because one is a Christian doesn't mean one is perfect."

She stretched out her arms. "I certainly am a good

example of that, me and my temper, at least where you're concerned."

The earl chuckled. "I do see. I promise to think on this, Angella. I will."

"This chestnut's a sweetgoer. So what happened to the whacking beast you claimed could beat me without blowing?" Angella laughingly called back to the earl.

Holding back his prime cattle, his gaze swept over the young woman whose wind-kissed cheeks flushed with triumph. He admired the picture she made in her warm black-and-silver frogged riding habit that showed off her young curves to advantage.

His hands tightened on the reins as the wind blew her hat akimbo on her head and streamed her hair down her back.

At the end of the long gallop, she pulled the chestnut to a walk, letting the earl, on his massive gray, ride up beside her. Unlike her, he wore a light cape over his Bishops' Blue riding jacket that fit him as though molded to his figure.

Her eyes danced mischievously as the earl moved alongside. With a terse smile on his face, he graciously admitted defeat. Angella challenged. "Smashing race. Want to do it again?"

"Smashing," agreed the earl, but declined. He wasn't about to explain to the girl, whose eyes lit with pleasure at besting him, that he held back his whacking beast on purpose. Though, not without some difficulty.

"You ride well."

"Father bought the best blood cattle he could afford. He believed a well-bred animal would give much better service than one with uncertain parentage. And my mother was a bang-up rider. She put us in the saddle practically before we could walk.

"Father kept only a couple of animals and a small carriage. I'm afraid I had to sell everything to pay for medicine and other expenses when they were ill." She sighed.

The earl enjoyed watching the picture Angella made riding his prime cattle. The docile plodders so popular among the ladies of the haute ton were not for her. She handled his cattle with an expertise most of his acquaintances would envy.

When he first took her to his stables, he hadn't expected her to respond with such enthusiasm. She took easily to the more cerebral pursuits of reading and study. He knew her to be a modest young woman of intelligence and wit, but he had no idea she was more than a bluestocking—in the best sense of the word.

He also found her compassionate, but firm with staff. Not once had he heard her raise her voice in anger. His lips twisted in a wry smile as he added silently, *Toward a servant anyway.*

Truth to tell, he thought he had her pretty well figured out until she saw his horses where, without an ounce of fear, she walked right up to the most unmanageable of his animals. With soothing voice and gentle hand, she quickly calmed the nervous animal. The change in the stallion's demeanor was nothing short of amazing.

"That was a ninnyhammer thing to do," he scolded her, "going right up to Apollo like that. He isn't known for his manners. You might have been seriously injured, or worse."

Her gaze narrowed and he tensed, waiting for the

explosion. Instead, she smiled sweetly as she rubbed the nose of the large horse who nudged her chest, asking for more attention. "Unlike some human beings, Apollo would never purposely injure me. Horses are more sensible, and, I might add, more sensitive than many people."

"Are you referring to me?" She grimaced in response to the scowl on his face. "I...I didn't mean...this time."

Slowly counting to ten, the earl growled. "And only caper-witted humans rush in where angels fear to tread."

Sorry," said Angella. As usual, her large repentant eyes charmed him, and the earl found his irritation fading. No matter what her offense, she was quick to apologize. When accompanied by her captivating hesitant smile, the earl was hard put not to give in to her. The little minx!

The next few days it looked as though the earl and Angella had left behind their disputes. As he claimed, he was a gentleman. She sensed he held himself in utmost control, not once stepping over the bounds into impropriety. She found her feelings for him growing stronger because of his self-restraint.

As they slowly rode side by side admiring the view of the half-frozen lake, the earl broached the subject again. "Angella. I talked to the Lord last night." A muscle in his cheek twitched. "I...uh...asked for your faith."

Joy radiated from her face. "Oh, Spensor, that's wonderful!" Reaching over, she touched his arm.

"I don't feel any different," he confessed. "Mayhap He did not accept a reformed rake."

"Of course He did," she assured him. "Trusting

Christ is more than emotion. It's a choice." She smiled. "Things will become different with time. You'll see."

He grinned with relief. "Telling you was more difficult than telling Father I wanted to fight Boney."

"I didn't know you…"

He cut her off. "I didn't. He forbade me to go, because I was his only heir. My best friend went. He was killed."

"You feel guilty for obeying your father."

"Put like that, it doesn't seem quite the same."

"Of course not, Spensor. Not everyone has been called to fight with the military. But God can take away that guilt if you ask Him. You're His child now."

As they talked, they turned their horses toward home. At the front of the manor, the earl lifted Angella from the saddle and escorted her into the hall. Benson took their capes and hats. "There are visitors in the blue parlor," he said. Angella heard disapproval and something more she couldn't figure out, in his tone.

Puzzled, Angella followed the earl into the wide room with its blue silk walls and blue-velvet-covered Queen Anne furnishings. A gaunt man stood in front of the hearth beside a shorter almost boyish-looking dandy at his side. Her eyes widened at the tall woman coming toward them, hands outstretched.

"Spensor. My darling Spensor, how could you leave me alone so long in London? Since you would not come to me, I had to come to you." She laughed. "You know, we have wedding plans to make."

Chapter 6

Against the elegance of the unexpected guests, Angella felt decidedly dowdy with her windblown hair tumbling over her shoulders, her hem damp and her half boots smudged with mud. As for the gaunt man by the hearth, she'd seen that look of animal lust before—in the eyes of the vicar. Fear knotted the pit of her stomach, fear and a certain despair.

Despite it all, Angella managed a polite but distant smile for the woman who took possession of the man who so recently said he cared for her. For a moment, Angella thought wildly, *It's all a mistake. Spensor will put the encroaching woman in her place and everything will be all right.*

But he didn't. The earl did nothing to disentangle himself from the woman's arms. As though he had no mind of his own, he allowed that woman to drag him to the sofa. He flashed Angella a look of total dejection, a silent apology that choked her. In that moment her heart broke.

The man tried to take her arm, but Angella deftly avoided him, hurrying to sit in a chair close to the sofa. Though the earl frowned, he but nodded her way as he sat opposite in a settee with his betrothed. He was betrothed!

The earl witnessed the glitter in Margaret's eyes as she scrutinized Angella's disheveled, but fashionable attire. "Darling," she crooned, "you didn't mention you were going to be entertaining a young woman at Lucashire." There was no mistaking the venom in her tone.

Helpless to halt the direction of Angella's thoughts or to derail Margaret's ire, the earl ground his teeth. Why did she have to show up now and without warning? No, 'twas his fault alone. He should have broken off with Lady Margaret long since.

Now Angella refused to meet his pleading gaze. Though she averted her face, he sensed her suffering as if it were his own. *Lord, help me,* he cried silently.

"Lady Margaret Ainsworth, may I make you known to my ward, Miss Angella Denning. Lord Hinton, Miss Denning. Herbert…Mr. Hinton, Miss Denning." Everyone made a pretense of civility.

"Surely she has not been living here unchaperoned, darling, has she?" At the earl's reluctant nod, Margaret patted his arm, her smile patently false. "Spensor, darling, whatever were you thinking? If she is an innocent, her reputation will be in shreds when the ton gets wind of her staying alone with such a virile bachelor."

The earl started at her implied threat. Why hadn't

he acted as soon as he realized he'd made a mistake on not seeking a companion for Angella? He well knew into what category Margaret now placed Angella, and it was his fault.

"Miss Denning," he said repressively, "has only recently become my ward. There is time, yet, to find a proper chaperone." As he reused the term, Angella winced. She didn't deserve this latest blow, but the earl was hard-pressed at the moment to know what else to do. Somehow he must deal with Margaret before mending his fences with Angella.

In his selfishness, he placed himself in an untenable position, never thinking of what he might be doing to Angella. If only things had worked out as planned. He owned he hadn't planned just what he was going to do about Margaret and now it might well be too late.

Sure he fully intended to make his break with Margaret, but had no notion how to go about it without causing a scandal that would reverberate not only on him, but also on Angella and Lady Margaret herself. How could he know Margaret would hunt him down in Lucashire?

"Miss Denning is the daughter of one of my vicars. He recently passed on, leaving her in my care."

Margaret rolled her eyes, taking no pains to hide her belief that she thought the girl beneath contempt. "One's people will take advantage if not kept down. Can you imagine foisting the chit on you in such a fashion?"

Angella whitened with mortification and anger, but held her peace, wishing a hole would open up in the floor for her to hide in. Margaret was not finished. "Darling, what are you going to do about her? You cannot keep her here. It isn't done. Surely you have some—"

she paused, then emphasized "—*distant* connection in need of a companion…or a governess. Though, she looks a bit young for that." She stared through Angella with contempt.

Clenching her hands to keep from slapping the woman, Angella wanted nothing more than to wipe the scorn from the other woman's face. Her own paled. The day disintegrated from there. Between Margaret's deliberate slights and Lord Hinton's familiarity, Angella fled to her bedchamber with relief.

Pounding her pillow, she cried, "I wish I didn't have to leave my room until they leave." She slumped. Little hope of that, not with Spensor—the earl—allowing all sorts of liberties of his person.

With his fiancée hanging on him every moment, there had been no opportunity for private conversation. No doubt, Margaret wanted to make certain the earl didn't stray again. Sarcasm twisted Angella's lips. Why should she wish to speak with Spen… The earl? Everything was clear enough. Anger gave way to deep, wrenching hurt.

She saw the devastating scene in a series of pictures: Lady Margaret's gushing display of affection, the earl's dismay, the vacuous grin of Herbert Hinton. Most of all, she shuddered at the leer on the face of Harry, Lord Hinton, Lady Margaret's brother, as he languidly surveyed her from top to bottom like a side of meat. His insolence infuriated her as it discomfited her.

"Lord, where is Edward? Is he ever coming home?" What if he didn't want to come home? That insidious thought was lowering in the extreme. Or couldn't! "Lord?"

Taking a deep breath, Angella started down the long

flowing staircase. Her hand gripped the warm smooth banister as she reluctantly descended the stairs.

The day had severely tried her emotionally. For a time, she considered pleading a megrim and excusing herself from the dinner party. It would not be entirely a whisker, but the pain lay in her heart, not in her head.

How could Spensor, Lord Lucashire, have so deceived her? She sighed at the possibility of love she had envisioned between herself and the earl. She saw them walking together, hand in hand, through life's changing seasons. Did she, a vicar's daughter, think the earl would actually consider marriage? What fustian! Such a green goose. No wonder Margaret looked down on her.

In one moment all her dreams, all her hopes had crashed. If his profession of caring was a sham, was his profession of faith any less? That pained more than the first. Swallowing the lump in her throat, Angella wiped a tear that insisted on blurring her vision. Spensor prattled on about honesty, about trust. What did the man know about either? She had been right to be suspicious of his motives. Yet, a voice inside reminded her he had not shamed her. Angella shook her head. It was so confusing. All she knew was that she needed to take herself in hand and expect nothing from her reluctant guardian.

How could everything continue so normally? Giggling maids hurried past, their arms loaded with brush and broom. A straight-shouldered footman caught up with the young maids. Whispering to them, he made them blush and giggle even harder.

How young they all seemed. Angella felt she'd aged considerably during the day. How naive she had been. How foolish. But then, she could not have known about the beautiful Lady Margaret. Now, there, she thought cynically, was the sort of woman she guessed would appeal to the appetites of a man like Lucashire.

When she entered the anteroom to the formal dining hall for dinner, Angella was hard put to force a polite smile. Lord Hinton was quick to acknowledge her presence.

Taking her hand, he led her farther into the room. "Miss Denning—Angella, if I may—you bring a breath of fresh air into this mausoleum." She felt his clammy wet palm through the silk of her rose gown.

"Miss Denning, if you please." She wasn't about to encourage him.

He laughed as though she jested, his pointed chin dropping onto his chest, making his thin face almost a caricature of himself. More off-putting than his features was the look in his eyes and the feel of his hands.

As Angella edged away, he pulled her back to his side. "None of that, Angella. Why, we're almost family." His glance took in his sister on the earl's rigid arm. "At least we'll soon be kissin' cousins so to speak. No Lord Hinton, now. The name's Harry."

Scrambling to her other side, Herbert added. "I am Herbert, pretty lady. You smell clean."

For a moment Angella panicked, but then she forced herself to think rationally. The younger brother seemed harmless enough. As she watched him parroting his older brother, Angella felt a certain sadness for the slow-witted man. To hide her irrational fear of Herbert, Angella smiled at him. "Thank you, Herbert."

The man positively beamed. "Herbert. She called me Herbert. Angella, Herbert. Herbert, Angella," he chanted until his brother shushed him.

Irritated, Lord Hinton proceeded to regale her with the wonders of London from the dark Tower of London to the in-demand, dignified actor John Kemble of Covent Garden.

"He's a sight to behold. Kemble is a good actor, though rather staid and unbending." Hinton continued despite Angella's inattention. "On the other hand, Kean makes quite the Shylock. Ah, yes, quite the villain." His leer crawled up Angella's skin like something living.

Too bad, she thought ruefully, *I didn't have protection against the earl's wiles.*

To her relief, Benson announced dinner. On Hinton's arm, she followed her erstwhile guardian and his chattering fiancée into the grand dining hall. Its magnificence overwhelmed her as it had since her first sight of the vaulted ceiling.

The table, smelling of beeswax and lemon, gleamed with its recent polishing until it reflected the gold-plated dinnerware and the sparkling silver embossed with the Lucashire crest. Waterford crystal goblets waited at each place.

Large bowls of fresh flowers decorated the table, adding a delicious fragrance to the delectable smells of the platters of food carried in on large trays by tall, well-built footmen in red-and-gold livery.

Gold-based candelabra lit the table, sending a soft glow over each face. Angella noted the earl looked particularly glum. His lips twisted cynically when he leaned forward as Lady Margaret whispered in his ear. His gaze caught Angella's, but she glanced away.

If he was out of countenance, so was she, thought Angella, shoving the food around on her plate without eating but a bite of this and that.

It didn't help to be derided by the London sophisticate when the footman brought Angella juice instead of wine. "My, my, child. How droll? What was your father anyway?"

"Leave her be, Margaret," commanded the earl, his tone sharp.

With a warning glance toward his sister, Hinton smoothed his sister's rudeness. "Let the chit drink what she pleases, Margaret." He hoisted his glass toward Angella. "Never fear, I shall take up the slack."

There was no doubt he did just that. Angella's eyes widened in amazement at the prodigious amount of spirits the gentleman managed to down without showing the least effect. Until dessert was served, that is. By that time, his speech slurred and the hand holding the goblet shook.

On the other side of her, Herbert—trying to keep up with his brother—tipped his own glass with increasing frequency. Margaret brought the interminable dinner to an end by rising to her feet. "Time we ladies excused ourselves," she said, patting the earl's arm. "Don't be too long, darling."

The earl scowled. Herbert giggled. Lord Hinton raised his glass and leered at Angella. "Nothing will keep me away long."

Throwing Lord Hinton a look of utter disgust, Angella rose to follow Margaret from the room.

Margaret walked down the long hall to the formal drawing room. There was no comfortable coz in the library that night. "Thank You, Lord," Angella breathed. The library held too many dear memories.

Though mostly healed, tonight her knee ached and Angella slowed to keep herself from falling as she followed the arrogant woman. In the torchlight, the red brocade on the walls glowed eerily. The statues seemed to move in the flickering light. Angella wished Lady Margaret had picked another room in which to retire after dinner. At least she had a short respite from the unwanted attentions of Lord Hinton.

Settling onto a long sofa, Margaret carefully arranged her skirts while studiously ignoring the younger woman. Surveying the elegant room with satisfaction, Angella heard her murmur, "Soon. Soon all this will be mine." Angella gritted her teeth to keep from screaming.

The stress of the day had taken its toll and, by the time the gentlemen condescended to attend them, Angella, in truth, had a nagging headache. Never had she thought she would be so thankful for pain. Pleading a megrim, she escaped to her bedchamber.

Anger welled up inside. Her prayers sounded more like accusations and dropped like lead from the ceiling. Her anger spent, her prayers turned toward her own attitude. "Lord, forgive me for my temper again. I get in a spin over the littlest things, but this isn't little, Lord. This is my life."

The next morning, as was her wont, Angella, dressed in a royal-blue riding habit edged in gold braid, descended the stairs, anticipating—as usual—a quiet ride with the earl. Despite his treachery in not telling her about Margaret, her heart pounded at the very thought of being with him.

In the quiet of her chamber the night before, she searched her own soul. She went to sleep with the sure knowledge that God had not forsaken her. In the newness of the morning, things didn't look so black. To own the truth, the earl had not shown particular affection toward his fiancée. But then, he had been caught out. Nonetheless, Angella was willing to listen to his explanation—if he had one. She so hoped he could explain. She so wanted him not to be the rake she first thought him to be.

However, instead of seeing the earl awaiting her, Angella came down to the great hall to find Lady Margaret and her brothers dressed to the nines for riding. Hinton held a silver riding crop that he impatiently slapped against his highly polished Hessian boots with their gold tassels.

Looking up, he saw Angella on the stairs and came to assist her. "Here she is. Now we're ready." Unable to come up with any way to avoid him, Angella allowed him to escort her out the front entrance where stable boys held the restless horses.

Sighing, Angella gave up on having a private word with her erstwhile guardian. Worse, as soon as she saw Angella pet the tall chestnut, who nuzzled her in return, Margaret demanded, "I want to ride that horse." She pointed to the chestnut, somehow aware of Angella's attachment to the animal.

"Prime cattle, Spensor. What's his name?"

"Cherry, Margaret." He snapped. "Angella usually rides him. Now, this is the animal I had brought around for you."

Her gaze narrow, Margaret interrupted him. "Darling, I want to ride this magnificent beast." She moved toward the side of the chestnut. "Come, Spensor, give me a hand up."

Angella waited for the earl to protest. Instead, without a word, he strode to Margaret's side and lifted her into the saddle. The triumph on the woman's face sickened Angella almost as much as the earl's silence.

Slowly she moved toward the steady but showy gelding more appropriate for an uncertain rider. The beautiful dapple gray would have shown off Lady Margaret's black-and-gold riding habit. If this was the mount chosen for Margaret, the earl thought little of her riding abilities. So why was he letting the woman ride Cherry, with his sensitive mouth?

Arranging Margaret's skirt over the pommel, the earl tried to get her to change her mind. "Margaret, Cherry will not do by half for you. Look, the gray will show your ensemble to greater advantage."

For a moment, Margaret pursed her lips as though about to change her mind—until she saw the set of Angella's shoulders. "Poo. Surely if she can ride the beast, I can."

Angella waited for the earl to take her part. Instead he shrugged and threw himself onto his mount without use of the stirrup.

Hinton reached to put her into the saddle, but Angella, feeling perverse, managed to outmaneuver him, giving Herbert the privilege. With a gurgle of excitement, he heaved her onto the saddle with so much force she would have gone on over if the earl had not grabbed her and settled her securely onto her mount. His gentleness stirred her and for a moment, she stared into his despairing eyes.

Obviously, Lady Margaret planned on taking control of the outing. Unfortunately, she didn't understand how to manage a spirited animal like Cherry and tugged at the animal's sensitive mouth. Angella flinched. The woman had little control of the animal, who balked or ran at his own volition, keeping the earl occupied with controlling the horse.

Angella fared little better. On one side Hinton paid her outrageously familiar compliments, while on the other side, Herbert babbled his appreciation. Time and again Herbert reached out to touch her arm, her face, her hair. His attentions unnerved her as Hinton's distressed her. Long before they returned, Angella vowed never to ride again with the motley crew.

Time and again in the days to follow, she tried to avoid not only the earl, but the scornful patronizing Lady Margaret, the lustful Lord Hinton and his unlikely mimic, Herbert, who parroted his brother's attempts at seduction, but with even less success. Hinton did the pretty, always attentive, always taking her hand, always whispering in her ear things which put her to blush.

Nothing she did discouraged the bounder in the least. If the earl realized she was uncomfortable, he gave no sign. Mayhap he just did not care. In Angella's mind, it amounted to the same thing.

A sennight later, she'd had enough. Pleading exhaustion, Angella excused herself from dinner. She could not force herself to sit through another meal with Lord Hinton's hand groping her knee under the table, could not stand one more evening having him paw her, one more evening watching Lady Margaret fawn over Spensor.

As she waited for darkness, her black kitten, considerably larger and sleek from eating well, scratched at her door. Opening it, Angella picked her up and buried her face in the cat's soft fur. "I have to leave," she told the kitten.

The cat meowed. Angella smiled as the kitten rubbed her cheek as though in understanding.

"Don't worry, little one, I'll leave you here where you have a good home." After a quick hug, she set the cat on the bed. With a wide yawn, the animal pawed the quilt, stretched then lay down and curled into a fluffy ball. A moment later her loud purrs punctuated the silence of the room.

Reluctantly, Angella donned a wool gown and drew a warm cape around her shoulders. From her window, she viewed the idyllic scene below. A full moon overhead shot silvery beams onto the snow below, lighting the path and deepening the shadows. The newly fallen snow, though pristine, looked hostile and cold.

Silently, Angella sneaked down the hall, down a back stairway to a little-used outside door. The bolts, though not used often, were kept oiled and in good repair. It was the work of a moment to pull the bolts and slip outside.

Skirting the large house and stables, Angella scurried into the shadows. Deep inside, she felt a disquiet about leaving, a silent disapproval. *What else can I do?* she cried silently into the looming darkness of the trees.

Praying no one watched from the grand windows of the salon above, Angella trudged through the thin layer of snow, toward the bridge. As much as possible she kept to the shadows. But glancing back, she felt her heart quail at the clear trail of footprints she left behind. "Lord, send more snow. Please cover those tracks before morning. I don't want him to fetch me back. Not this time."

Not that she had any idea of where she was going. In her satchel, she had a single gold piece the earl insisted she have for her work in the library. She hoped it would get her a ride to some town where she might find work. And if she froze in the night? Her sigh escaped in a white cloud. Who would care? As for Hinton, she shuddered.

His whispered suggestions had become more and more vulgar and his hands more and more familiar with each passing day. Obviously, he thought her fair game, and who was there to gainsay him? Certainly not the earl, she thought with newfound cynicism.

Angella shuddered as she pulled the cape more closely around her shoulders. Lord Hinton took few pains to keep his lust for her secret from his brother whose own attentions had become more familiar. As Angella reached the bridge, she thought that however bad the future, she was well shot of Lucashire. Only the thought of the earl twisted painfully inside.

Grasping the ice-covered rail, Angella moved slowly over the bridge. Suddenly, long arms grabbed her and swung her off her feet. She gasped as she stared up into the face of the earl. There was no doubt that this time he was in a towering rage.

Chapter 7

In all his life the earl had not had to deal with a situation that affected him so dearly. Never had he cared so passionately for the outcome. The most surprising of all to him was that he was more concerned for Angella than for himself. That, more than all else, showed him the validity of his new faith.

Questions burned in his mind. What must Angella think of him? What disillusionment must she be going through?

In the parlor, he got up from the sofa, where he was sitting beside Margaret, to pace the room. He had seen the effort Angella made to comport herself like a lady in the face of Margaret's patent snobbery. Fact was, Angella showed herself every bit a lady, unlike his "fiancée." He recalled his fears that Angella would not know how to behave in polite company. If one could call

Margaret and her brothers polite company. He ground his teeth. They were anything but, and he wished them any place but in his ancestral home. He had been mistaken about Angella in so many ways. If nothing else, Margaret's arrival showed him the arrogant man he had become. He did not blame Angella for not wanting to be in their presence—nor his. He winced.

Moving to the window, he drew aside the heavy velvet winter curtains to look out toward the front of the hall. The snow sifted pristine and white over the bushes, the last of the flowers, covered the trees like goose down and gave the bridge an ethereal appearance as though it were emerging from the nether regions. The surface would be icy, he knew, and he reminded himself to have Benson ask the servants to clear it at first light.

No, he did not blame Angella for avoiding the after-dinner tête-à-tête. He cared not much for it himself. Besides Margaret's efforts to make a cake of Angella, he was also aware of Angella's attempts to fend off the lecherous Lord Hinton. The earl clenched his teeth in frustration.

That very forenoon he had again cautioned Harry. "I will not have you frightening the girl, so keep your hands off her."

A slow smile had played at the corners of Harry's mouth. "You have your cozy armful, so leave me to my entertainment. There is little enough to do in this godforsaken place. Besides, it is a trifle, a mere harmless flirtation."

"If you overstep your bounds, I vow you'll find yourself married to Miss Denning. I'll not have you trifle with her affections." From the look of amusement on Harry's face, the earl well knew the man sensed he had no intention of forcing him to come up to scratch. Even the thought turned his stomach.

Hinton's indifference to the earl's warnings vexed him to no end. His prospective brother-in-law sensed Spensor's tendre for his ward and played upon that affection. Bother! He would never force Angella to marry the bounder. Lord Hinton wasn't good enough for her by half.

Still and all, the earl found himself feeling not so much hatred for Margaret and her brothers but frustration and a certain sadness. He thought back to that fateful night in London. The earl recalled dancing with Margaret, then others claiming his attention; recalled wandering off to the card room and sitting in on a friendly game. As always he took care not to bet too deeply nor lose too heavily, as did others far more gone in their cups.

What he did *not* recall was imbibing as deeply as Margaret later claimed he had. Toward dawn as the crowd thinned, the game broke up and he went to find Margaret.

He'd grown bored with the London round...and with Margaret.

Nonetheless he bowed as she said, "Dance with me once more, Spensor, before the orchestra packs up and leaves." Taking her into his arms, he moved with her around the floor. Already, streaks of dawn filtered through the edges of the brocade curtains.

As the music faded, he led his companion to the side. Harry stood at the table with another glass in hand. "Been a long night, old chap." He shoved the drink into the earl's hand. "Merely lemonade. Drink up."

Thirsty, the earl accepted the drink and tossed it

down his throat. Handing back the glass, he said with finality, "I must be going." He smiled. Harry smiled back at him. Herbert grinned. He felt decidedly odd.

Margaret, however, frowned. "Oh, darling, not yet."

Things got fuzzy after that, but somehow before he left he found himself engaged to Margaret, tied forever to her and her leech of a brother. Much later, he wondered about the drinks supplied at every turn by the ever-smiling Harry. There was something havey-cavey about the whole thing, but how could he prove it? Besides, by then it was too late. Much, much too late. A day later he sought some way to call off the engagement.

Looking inside himself now, he had to admit, with some surprise, he had changed since then. Angella was right, as usual, even about his untested faith. It stretched within him strong and resilient, like new rope. Was Margaret's coming a testing of that faith?

Glancing out the window, he tensed as a shadow moved beneath the snow-laden pine and oak. The shadows shifted. Nothing more. No, there it was again. Shielding his eyes from the light reflecting on the panes, the earl peered into the darkness.

Furtively, a shadow moved into the silvery moonlight. Detached from the trees, the shadow took human shape, female shape. Angella! In the bright moonlight he recognized the cape and the determined set of those shoulders as she trudged through the snow. What was she about now?

With an oath he immediately regretted, he swung about. Flinging back a short apology, he raced from the room. Not waiting to don coat or hat, he ran through the door of the great hall and out into the cold night.

Angella had no notion of the treachery of the bridge

in winter as did he. Snow oozed over his evening pumps, soaking his feet as he raced to intercept Angella before she reached the bridge. The goose-witted girl was at it again. Whyever did she pick this night of all nights to run off? His lungs ached from his sprint to rescue Angella. Too late. She reached the bridge.

"What's the matter with you?" he yelled. Leaping onto the bridge behind her, he swung her up into his arms. Clutching her to his chest, he moved carefully but quickly away from the icy bridge. "Have you bats in the cockloft," he scolded, "running off like that in the middle of the night!"

"Oh, put me down." Angella squirmed in his grasp, but he grimly held on to her. "You have no right to detain me, m'lord. Now, put me down!"

"Be still, girl. However much you hate me, if you will not be still, we shall both go down and break our fool necks. Or haven't you noticed the undercoating of ice? The bridge is thick with it."

"I'll be fine. Let me go."

"Fool girl. That bridge is a death trap in this weather. No one can safely negotiate it until the ice is removed. You'd die trying to cross."

Tears froze on her cold cheeks. "At least I'd be with those who love me."

Stung, the earl held her closer. "You want to take me with you?"

Angella stopped struggling, her body rigid in his arms. The earl muttered under his breath. It was freezing cold and it seeped inside his thin dinner jacket to chill his skin. He held Angella close as much for her warmth as to secure her in his grip.

Angella put her arms about his neck. "You shouldn't

have come out in this weather without a coat. You should not have come after me at all. You'll probably catch your death." He did not miss her anxiety and it sparked hope within him.

A smile touched his face for the first time in days. He felt giddy with a happiness he knew would not last, not until he solved his problem with Margaret. It felt good to hold his Angella in his arms. His Angella? He slowed his pace. Despite the biting chill of the wind, the earl relished the feel of the young woman against him—where she belonged.

"Whyever did you run away, Angella? I know you've had a shock, more than one, but this, this is daft. We need to talk, I know. Surely you could have come to me?"

"When? How? Certainly not with Lady Margaret all over you, cooing in your face. She hasn't let you off her leading string since she arrived."

The earl grimaced at her apt description. "Don't I know, but…this was a hen-witted thing to do. You may not believe this, but I care what happens to you, Angella."

"Sure you do. That's why you forgot to mention you already had a fiancée. That's why you've ignored me all week, taking her part in everything. Of course, that is as it should be since *she* is your intended." Angella gulped. "I should hate you. I should."

"But you don't?" The earl wasn't sure how to deal with that realization.

"No. I want to, but no." Angella coughed before continuing. "I'm hurt and angry, but you're miserable, as well. Still…"

The earl slipped, caught his balance and continued

toward the hall. "You must let me explain. But you need to explain this hen-witted caper, as well." Ice from overhead trees showered down on them. "Why must you always run away?"

"You must understand that I saw no other choice." Angella sighed. "I had to get away!" she cried. "I knew not what else to do. Harry is overfamiliar and I cannot stop him. Lady Margaret never misses a chance to set me down, and you…you have been acting like an odious, hypocritical, treacherous bounder who…who…" She stopped. He heard the sob in her voice.

Her accusations hurt more than ever Angella could know. He who despised dishonesty and hypocrisy turned out to be the worst offender of all. "I know all that and I'm sorry, but what would you have me do now?"

Angella heard genuine hopelessness in his tone that effectively checked her desire to hurt him as he had hurt her. Had she not once planned on giving him opportunity to explain without prejudice? But that was over a week ago. He'd made no attempt to explain to *her*. Still and all…

"I'd like to hear you out, Spensor," she told him. Inside she felt a sense of peace.

Hugging her, the earl carried her up the steps into the great hall. Angella shook with cold and the earl shivered, but he refused to set her down until he reached one of the two ancient fireplaces on either end of the hall. During the days of knights and maidens fair, whole oxen had been turned on spits in the massive hearths. Now the roaring fire shot its heat toward them as the earl set Angella on a long settee before the fire and sat beside her.

Unfastening her cape with stiff shaking fingers, he slid it off her shoulders. Mrs. Karry hovered near, offering hot chocolate. Benson took the cape without a word, exchanging it for a warm blanket. The earl was handed a dry, informal jacket, which he slipped on over his damp shirt. He slid out of his shoes into slippers brought for him.

The mug warmed Angella's hands. With a sigh, she sipped the hot liquid, letting it slide deliciously down her throat. The earl sipped his chocolate, as well. Silence reigned as they let the fire and the beverage warm them inside and out. Beside her, the earl leaned back, echoing her sigh.

Angella exchanged a shy glance with the earl. There was no doubt he felt as awkward as she. Angella's kitten leaped onto her lap, demanding attention.

Laughing, Angella set down her cup and hugged the growing kitten to her red cheeks. "Did you miss me so soon?" She smoothed the kitten's fur. The cat's big round green-yellow eyes looked at her without blinking. Then she settled down in Angella's lap. In the quiet with the only sounds the crackle of the fire and the low murmur of the butler giving directions in the background, Angella relaxed. Reaching over, the earl scratched the kitten's ears. He and Angella smiled hesitantly at each other.

The comfortable bond between them broke at the strident voice behind them. "There you are, darling. Whyever did you go running off like that?"

Coming up to them, Margaret, without a by-your-leave, wedged herself between the earl and Angella.

A moment later, she leaped to her feet with a squeak of alarm. "Why, you're damp." She made it sound like some loathsome disease.

Her gaze narrowed as it moved from Angella to the earl. "What's going on, darling?" For the first time she noticed the cat staring up at her from Angella's lap. "That cat. It's black!"

At the tone of her voice, the kitten hunched its back and hissed at her, preparing to leap. Margaret stepped back. "Get that cat out of here," she screeched.

"What's this?" Harry came up beside his sister followed, of course, by Herbert.

Herbert reached down to touch the cat. "Nice kitty."

His sister slapped his hand away. "No, Herbert. Don't touch that cat."

Fearfully he tucked his hands behind his back.

"Stop being an addlepate, Margaret." Harry laughed. "It is only a cat, sis. Don't frighten Herbert." He viewed the animal dubiously.

"It's merely Miss Denning's pet," the earl said. "There is nothing intrinsically evil about a color."

Keeping her eye on the beast, who continued to stare at her, Margaret nervously settled into a nearby chair. "Darling, were you effecting a midnight rescue or a rendezvous at this time of the night?" There was deadly undertone to her polite inquiry.

The earl hesitated. "I fear, Miss Denning decided to go for a walk to clear her head. Unfortunately, she has no idea how icy the bridge gets at this time of the year. When I saw her out the window, I knew I had no time to lose."

"Poor darling." Margaret sighed, before continuing. "Your little backcountry mouse is such a trial. We really must get her settled. Surely there is some tenant farmer or other mutton-headed coxcomb who wouldn't inquire too deeply into her unchaperoned activities under the care of the Earl of Lucashire."

"Margaret." Angella heard the earl's unspoken warning.

Clutching the kitten, Angella got to her feet. For a moment her tired knee threatened to buckle and she swayed. Herbert grabbed her before she fell. Angella flashed a smile at him. "Thank you, Herbert. That was most kind."

He beamed. "Pretty Angella. Pretty lady." He let her go reluctantly.

As though recognizing Angella was poised for flight, the earl also stood and took her arm. "Why don't we all return to the parlor." Both women shot him looks he ignored as he steered them all down the hall.

The earl managed to ensconce Angella next to himself, leaving both Harry and Margaret disconcerted. There was little warmth in the room other than that from the hearth as each avoided looking at the other. First the earl, then Harry, valiantly tried to introduce subjects for conversation, but discussion quickly died in the tension between the two women.

The earl's ragged cough galvanized both Margaret and Angella into action. Starting to her feet, Margaret exclaimed, "Spensor, see what a fool thing you did going out like that. You should have sent a flunky to get her, instead of playing the gallant yourself."

Frowning behind another cough, the earl shook his head. "No time." At Angella's gasp, he grabbed her hand. "I had to go."

Forcing a smile, Angella daintily tugged her fingers from his bone-crunching clasp. "You need to go to bed."

Throwing a malevolent glance toward Angella, Margaret took the earl's arm. "Unfortunately, she is right. You must take care of yourself. I'll not be having you catch your death."

"I am not feeling quite the thing," the earl said, acquiescing with a sharp nod. "I do feel rather chilled." With that, he hied himself off to his rooms.

With his departure, Margaret dismissed Herbert, also, as one would send off a child. "You, too, Herbert. Time for bed."

"Aw, I want to stay with the pretty lady."

Margaret's expression grew stern. "Not now, Herbert. Maybe…later." Lord Hinton backed her up, his predatory gaze on Angella.

Grunting, Herbert got up and lumbered from the room.

Angella picked up the kitten and prepared to depart for the peace and security of her bedchamber.

"Miss Denning, I hope you'll remember that whatever relations you may have had with my fiancé, he is pledged to me. He may have his lightskirts, that I fully expect, but I will not have them in my home. Do we understand one another?"

Biting her lip, Angella held her peace as she mouthed polite platitudes of escape. Nothing she said would convince Margaret of the truth of the matter, so why try?

"I'm glad we understand one another." Margaret smiled, then said, "We'll see to your future, never fear."

Angella left with all the dignity she could muster.

In the hall, the kitten meowed loudly and jumped from Angella's arms. Angella followed the kitten, who mischievously edged open the door next to the parlor where they had been sitting. The unused room was cold and dark, with only a sliver of light coming in from the partially open door between the rooms.

The luminous eyes of the kitten blinked at her from under a claw-footed chair. Cautiously, Angella tracked the kitten, who danced away on her little cat feet as though playing a game. "Come here," whispered Angella, making a grab for her. She missed.

The kitten blinked at her again before leaping toward the door. In desperation, Angella leaped after her, catching her just before she scampered into the parlor. Voices sounded from the other room, harsh accusing voices. Then she heard her name. Clutching the kitten to her chest, Angella froze.

"We must do something about the girl, Margaret, and don't expect me to come up to scratch. I have much higher expectations than Spensor's cast-off doxy, however charming. Now, if she had a hefty portion..." Angella could almost see his cadaverous smile.

"Well, she doesn't. How was I to know he would fall for the likes of her? Besides, I'm not the one running from the duns."

"No, but I haven't got him in a taking by my rag manners, either. Haven't you more sense than to treat the girl as you do?"

"Poo. She's of no consequence. Once she's settled right and tight, I'll see to it that Spensor doesn't concern himself with her again. What we need do is find some suitable parti for her to wed."

"Right. In the middle of Kent. Girl or no girl, you have got to get the settlements signed to make this engagement official. It's not as though Spensor is besotted with your person, sis. if we hadn't made slight additions to his drinks that night, he would not now be—rather reluctantly, I might add—looking ahead to being hauled down to the altar." His long shadow stretched across the room toward the door as he paced. Gulping, Angella drew back, her eyes wide with discovery.

"You well know if I can't come up with the blunt in another week, the duns will have me in Fleet prison. With a scandal like that in the offing, how long do you think you'd hang on to your precious earl?"

"I know. I know. If only you could have lived within the credit we received on the strength of my coming nuptials. But no, as usual, off you go to lose, again, at the baize tables. You are just like father." She paused. "There has got to be a way…" Angella heard her sigh. "Wait a minute, I think…" Angella heard her rise. "Come, Harry, I have the very thing."

Shocked by what she had heard, Angella held her place until she could no longer hear footsteps in the hall. Then, clutching the kitten to her chest, she carefully made her way out of the darkened room and back into the hallway. Soon, safely ensconced in her bedchamber, she set down the kitten, who immediately leaped onto her bed and curled into a furry ball.

Needing time to assimilate what she had heard, Angella spoke little as the maid assisted her out of her gown and into a long nightdress. Crawling between the covers, she stretched her feet down to the wrapped brick heating the bed, careful not to dislodge the sleeping kitten.

Quietly the maid wished her good-night as she doused the candles. From past experience, she left the door slightly ajar so the kitten might leave in the night should she need to go down to the kitchen.

In the dark, Angella mulled the information she inadvertently overheard. From what Harry said, Spensor had been tricked into acknowledging Lady Margaret as his intended. Not too sporting, but then, the earl's deep pockets were well-known, and Harry was obviously both desperate and devious. Somehow, Angella knew she must find a way to speak to the earl in private to let him know the truth of the matter.

Hope rose. Hope died. It would make little difference. By whatever means the engagement came about, the earl was duty bound to marry the scheming woman.

As much as she wished to stay awake to think, the walk and the cold had taken its toll. Beside her the kitten's purr lulled her to sleep. Her eyes closed.

In her dreams she grimaced, moved. Suddenly she sat up. The heavy breathing was not a part of a dream, but close beside her. Fetid breath heated her face. Frightened now, she reached out to push away the hulking figure blocking the little light emanating from the embers in the hearth.

"Who are you? What do you want?"

Thick clammy hands touched her cheeks with surprising gentleness. Quelling panic, Angella struggled. "Go away. Leave me alone!"

A moment later hands grabbed at her in an awkward caress. She gasped, crying out in pain. "No! Leave me be."

A guttural boyish laugh met her plea. "I want you, pretty lady. You want Herbert. Sis say you want Herbert. Harry say you want Herbert. He want you. Herbert want you."

She felt his body plopping down beside her. Losing the last shred of control, Angella pushed him away, scratching and clawing at his face and arms. Grappling with the groping arms, Angella screamed and screamed again, only to have her screams cut off by a wet kiss that so revolted her she thought never to be clean again. The whole of it was obscene.

"God," she screamed. "Help me! Save me!"

Stirred from sleep, a small furry missile, angry at being disturbed, hurled herself at Herbert's face, claws extended. This time it was he who screamed as he tried to protect his face. As he grabbed for the elusive kitten, Angella threw the covers away from Herbert and slid to the floor. Grabbing her robe, she hurried across the floor in her bare feet. Behind her she heard a frightened meow, a hard thump and silence.

"Pretty lady hurt Herbert." She heard him come after her. Panicked, she slammed the door closed behind her. Pulling on the robe, which covered her like a warm blanket from neck to toes, she hurried down the hall as fast as she was able. At Spensor's study next to his bedchamber she spotted a dim light under the door. Grabbing the handle, she swung into the room.

Entering the room, she oriented herself by the flickering light of the fire. "Spensor," she whispered loudly. "Spensor help me!"

The earl, who had been sitting quietly before the fire reading instead of being in bed, shook his head as if to clear it. "Angella, what is it? What's wrong?" Setting aside his book, he got to his feet.

At the sound of his voice, a sob broke forth from her as she flung herself into his arms. "Spensor, oh Spensor. Herbert is after me. Margaret and Harry sent him to assault me in my own chambers." Then she wept.

"Lord in heaven." As his arms closed around Angella, she sensed his rage. Where was the loving Heavenly Father now?

Chapter 8

As the earl held the shivering girl for the second time that night, he wondered what time it might be. No light showed through the heavy curtains. He heard no sounds in the hall nor outside the window other than the wind.

Not being able to sleep, he'd gotten up to read. His cough disappeared as the heat warmed him. Fleetingly, he wondered if God had awakened him for this moment of Angella's need. *Oh, Lord!*

Much as he wanted to know exactly what that caper-witted Herbert had been about, he knew Angella was in no shape to explain further at the moment. Still, he must try to understand. Picking her up, he sat with her on the settee. "Now, tell me, Angella. What's wrong?" For a long time she clung to him, her eyes wide with near hysteria. Murmuring softly, the earl soothed her until the panic left her face and tears started in her eyes.

In the circle of his arms Angella sobbed out her fright and hurt of the past week. For a long time she wept, until she relaxed against him in sheer exhaustion. The earl kept his hold gentle. He didn't think she even realized he held her.

"Angella, whatever it is, it's all right. It's all right. I'll take care of you."

She stiffened and raised her head. In the dim light he watched the blush start across her cheeks as she tried to push herself away from his embrace.

"Be still, Angella. Think you so little of me that you assume I'd take advantage of you or anyone who came to me for safety?"

"No, no. You would not, but this is wrong. I shouldn't be here. I must go...."

"Where? No one is about, Angella, other than that dim-witted Herbert and he'd be far too frightened of me to follow you into my study." The earl held her to his side.

"Now, relax. I shall not hurt you."

"I shouldn't stay." She slurred her words.

"There, that's better," he said as she snuggled closer. "Now, tell me exactly what happened." He felt her tense again and tightened his hold.

"He came to my bedchamber."

"Herbert?" The earl gulped down anger and tried to remain calm for Angella's sake.

"Herbert, I never thought...never considered... I mean...Lord Hinton was always... Oh, you didn't know..." She paused, then gulped. "Or care..."

The earl managed to catch the gist of this. "Oh, Angella, I cautioned Harry numerous times to keep his lecherous hands off you."

Her face showed surprise. Did she really think he didn't notice or care?

Angella sucked in a breath. "He did not listen—ever. He was despicably vulgar. I didn't know how to fend him off. Nothing discouraged him."

"Is that why you ran away this evening?"

Angella shuddered. "Lord Hinton told me he was coming to my room."

Fury exploded in the earl's eyes. "He didn't."

"He did. I didn't know how else to escape him." She sniffed as tears began to once more trickle down her face.

"Angella, I am so sorry. Some protector I am." He deserved her condemnation. He'd been going along, trying to calm the situation. In doing so, he saw now, he'd let Angella down—again. "Oh, Lord—help!"

Wiping away the tears, Angella hiccuped, and continued. "What did they hope to accomplish by sending Herbert to my room?" She trembled at the memory.

"I can guess. They assumed I'd permit that dimwit to have you."

"You wouldn't?"

"I'll have him strung up for what he did." The earl sighed, wondering how to ask, then barged ahead. "What did he do, Angella?"

Angella sucked in a painful breath. "He tried to get into bed with me. His hands groped." She shook and her eyes revealed her revulsion. A hysterical giggle escaped her lips. "Believe it or not, 'twas the kitten who bought me time to get away. I prayed, you see, and suddenly the cat leaped at him. She was sleeping on the bed with me. When she attacked, I ran. But I think he killed her." She repeated with deep sadness, "I think he…he killed her."

"Maybe not. We'll check later." The earl studied her face. "You ran to me. Despite all the things that have happened, you ran to me."

"I had nowhere else to turn. But—" he felt her tense "—that changes nothing. Even if you were tricked into a betrothal with Lady Margaret, you should have told me."

"Tricked? What do you mean?" He straightened and stared down into her face. Mayhap there was hope. "How did you discover that? I daresay Margaret did not tell you. I had my suspicions, but…"

Angella hesitated. "I…uh…happened to overhear her and Harry talking. They didn't know I was in the next room chasing the cat." She paused before explaining further.

"The cat escaped, and I was trying to catch her. The connecting door between the rooms was open, and, well, I listened."

"Hush, you have no reason to justify eavesdropping, Angella. I'm glad you know. There never was much true feeling between us. What we had was much more basic, I fear."

"You didn't tell me about her. You let me think you cared…that, mayhap, there was a future…." She shook her head. "Was any of that true?"

Her distress brought a grimace to his lips. "I have come to care deeply for you, Angella. I just didn't know what to do about Margaret. I never considered the possibility that she might come here before I found a way out. Truly, I planned on confronting the situation."

"When? And what about your faith? Is it real, or just something to satisfy me?"

"Bother, Angella. I am well aware I've played the fool. I know I've hurt you deeply, and for that I take full blame. But I have not lied to you. I did not tell you all the truth, but my caring is real. My faith is real, too." He shrugged. "I needed time. You needed time to see what the future held for us. I did not want to make another mistake."

He allowed her to search his face as he continued. "You were right about faith, Angella. Because I have someone outside myself to go to with my problems, this coil with Margaret has been much less difficult to handle than it might have been. Truth to tell, had I not felt sorry, rather than furious, at Margaret, I would not have put up with them this long."

His arms tightened about her. "I've been trying to come up with some way to break this infernal betrothal without causing scandal. In the process, I hurt you, Angella, but what am I to do? I cannot marry that woman. She would never remain faithful to me long, and her brother... He is addicted to gambling, as well as to assorted other vices, one of which you are well aware."

"Yes, I know. I wanted to tell you. Harry told Margaret she must press to get the marriage settlements signed, because he's under the hatches so severely he fears he'll be in Fleet soon if you don't bail him out."

"Again. So that explains this surprise visit. I should have figured, since Margaret has been hinting at it all week. Of course, I wasn't about to fall for that, not when I was looking for a way out."

They were silent then, and Angella leaned against Spensor, wishing she could stay beside him, but knowing she must return to her own room. "I…can't stay here. But where can I go?" Angella shook her head

"I'll not permit Herbert to touch you again. Thank the Lord for that cat. Bother Herbert anyway. Never took him for that type. Not even with Harry's careful coaching."

"He… Herbert said they told him I wanted him. I don't think he realized I didn't… When the cat attacked, Herbert got very angry." She cringed and hid her face against the earl. "It was awful. The way he grabbed and kissed me. The…the way he touched me."

"Angella." It was a groan. "I can't. I won't permit you to return to your room with Herbert about. There is just no way to predict what he will do, especially if those two set him up. Stuff and nonsense!"

"I know," Angella whispered. "Margaret feared you would not marry her as long as I was about. She said she wanted to find someone to marry me. I suppose she thought if Herbert…" She shivered. "I could never… Not ever."

"He'd be no proper husband to any woman," growled the earl. "Only Margaret would think up such a diabolical plan. No, I'll not give you away, not to the likes of Herbert or Harry." Wrapping his arms around her, he held her close, resting his head on hers.

"Shh. I think I heard someone." Angella tensed, moved closer to him. She heard footsteps, then saw the handle turn.

The door squeaked as it slowly opened. Angella closed her eyes, expecting Herbert's bulk.

Instead she smelled cloying perfume. Margaret's scent drifted into the room ahead of her. The earl sounded amused as he greeted the woman who held aloft a thick bedchamber candle. "Good evening, Margaret. And what brings you out this night? Herbert, mayhap?"

"He said the girl came in here. Regular visitor I well imagine. I give you fair warning, Spensor. Have all the doxies you wish, but keep them elsewhere. I'll not have them fouling my nest."

The earl's lips tightened. "As usual, you mistake the situation. We all know the truth of the matter. Now, if you have nothing further to add, I suggest you let yourself out of my study and hie off to bed. You had better see that Herbert stays in his. Fair warning. If he does not, I'll see that slow-witted man put where he can no longer harm or frighten anyone."

Margaret puffed with anger. "How dare you! Herbert is my brother. It isn't his fault he had an accident that damaged him when he was in leading strings."

"Your concern for him is touching. Truth to tell, Herbert is probably the best of the lot of you, but not when you use him in your games. Good night, Margaret. Close the door on your way out."

"I'll see Angella back to her own chamber," Margaret suggested.

"No, she stays with me, where I can protect her from your wiles. Good night."

Seeing there was no gainsaying him, Margaret retreated with ill grace, slamming the door behind her.

"She'll think the worst of the situation," Angella began.

"You're thinking about that verse about avoiding the very appearance of evil?"

Angella nodded, surprised he knew the verse. The

reference fell automatically from her lips. "1 Thessalonians 5:22. Spensor, you've been reading your Bible."

He grinned. "Every day. I had no notion of all the wonderful things it contains."

Glancing away, Angella murmured, "Oh, Spensor. Here I've been condemning you, while I've been the one neglecting my devotional time. I let fear take over. I knew He didn't want me to run away again, but I did it anyway."

The earl tilted her chin so he might see her face. His eyes were soft with care. "Thank you for telling me that, Angella. Sometimes I worry that I am not good enough for my little saint."

Leaning against his shoulder, Angella whispered, "How can you say so. I'm no saint. You know my dreadful temper. But about staying with you…"

"Under the circumstances, I see nothing wrong with protecting you," he insisted. Getting up, he lifted her in his arms. Laying her down on the wide sofa, he found a blanket that he carefully tucked around her.

Kissing her forehead reverently, he smoothed a lock of hair from her still-damp cheek. "You'll be safe enough here. I'll be next door in my bedchamber. The door will be locked, but should you need anything, call."

"Margaret?" Angella yawned.

"Never mind her. I have, finally, thought of just the way to deal with her and Harry on the morrow." The earl gently ran his finger down her cheek. At the door, he turned.

"Go to sleep, Angella. I'll wake you up before the servants are astir and take you back to your room. No one but Margaret will ever be the wiser, and I can buy her silence."

The next morning, after an uneasy breakfast, the earl gathered his unwanted guests together in the library. He kept Angella close by his side, his eyes on the sullen Herbert, who had done nothing more than mumble since he tromped downstairs.

Angella avoided Herbert's gaze, focusing instead on his hastily tied cravat. Margaret's lips turned down peevishly as she idly tugged at the sash under her ample bosom. Harry, in the first stare of fashion as always, sat back nonchalantly, his face showing his amusement. The earl wore a forbidding frown.

The room was still as the unwanted guests waited to see what the earl would say. In the silence, the fire in the grate crackled loudly. Sunshine poured into the room from the windows edged with delicate ice lace.

With dispassion, the earl surveyed the woman who had tricked him. Yet was not the fault his, as well? In his own way, he used her as she used him. His lips tightened. "Margaret, it behooves me to inform you that I acknowledge my fault in our situation. Though our betrothal was not my intention at the time, and though you forced my hand by trickery, I am willing to go ahead with our marriage."

Beside him Angella gasped, her face whitened. Margaret, however, straightened. She shot Angella a glare of triumph, short-lived as the earl continued quietly.

"There are a few things we must clear up first. The first of which is that I wish you to understand I have paid off all the debts I plan on paying off for any member of your family, Margaret." His gaze caught the outrage on Margaret's face.

Abruptly the amusement faded from Hinton's eyes. "You can't do this. I need…"

"Indeed I can. I have financial responsibilities other than keeping you out of Fleet. It is long past time you stand on your own two feet, Harry. Be that as it may, I have another requirement, as well." He cleared his throat ominously. "Herbert is to be permanently corralled."

Margaret bristled. "I'll not send him to Bedlam. You know what that place is like. Herbert is not mad, just a bit slow."

"And dangerous when used in your petty manipulations." His expression hardened.

Margaret had the grace to look away. He sensed she was irritated more by failure than by her instigation of the action. "He would do well enough for the likes of a country flirt."

"Fustian! You have windmills in your head if you thought such a thing would succeed. Even the most reluctant of guardians would turn him down as a suitor. No title, no money and little mind. You but betrayed your own cause in this havey-cavey scheme."

Harry glowered at his sister as though it were all her fault. "Told you it was a half-cocked thing to do."

"Oh hush, you were willing enough to give Herbert particular instructions last night."

In confusion, Herbert looked from one to the other. "I hurt kitty." Sadness showed in his eyes. "Pretty Angella run away."

"That's right, Herbert. What you did was wrong." The earl looked at Harry and Margaret. "If Angella had not taken her kitten to her room, I assure you, Herbert would have found himself in much worse circumstances than Bedlam. I would have seen to that.

"But I am not suggesting anything as drastic as Bedlam, I am suggesting I find him a place and a companion outside your sphere of influence. I'm certain we could find something for him to do on one or another of my estates."

"Work!" shrieked Margaret. "How dare you. He's a gentleman!"

The earl smiled laconically. "*Work* is not such an obscene word, Margaret. Honest work certainly shows more integrity than gambling...or living off one's relatives." His steady gaze discomfited Harry.

"Bluffing, old chap." Harry forced cheerfulness. "Throwing a scare in us. Have it your way. Pay off and I'll take it easy at the tables."

"No. I do not bluff, Harry. If I marry Lady Margaret, you'll not see one penny piece of either her income, or mine. Trust me, I shall see to it she offers you nothing—not unless she wishes to find her own allowance cut off."

Margaret's face reddened. "You odious blackguard. We're betrothed. As a man of honor, you must go through with the wedding."

"I believe I made myself clear about fulfilling my obligations. My conditions, too, are clear."

For the first time since entering the room, the earl watched Angella begin to relax. He'd seen her bow her head and felt her prayers. When she glanced up at him, he also witnessed a look of peace and a trust in him that overwhelmed him. She was so innocent, so honest. With deliberation, he refocused on Margaret and her brothers.

"I have another solution."

Margaret and Harry exchanged a long look. "What is it?" Harry finally asked as the earl leaned back languidly, viewing them through narrowed eyes.

"Simply this. I will pay off all Harry's current debt, as well as offer a substantial settlement providing you, Margaret, call off the betrothal. The settlement would be large enough that, if you stay in the country and economize, you can live right well."

Margaret frowned. "You can't," she choked.

"Certainly I can. It's your choice, Margaret. See Harry in Fleet and Herbert working as a common laborer or call off the wedding."

Agitated, Margaret got to her feet. "If I let you go, all of the ton will know it's because of that lightskirt. If ever you try foisting her on society, she'll be shunned."

Vengeance sat heavy on her face.

"We'll see that doesn't happen." Inwardly the earl recoiled from the woman he had once thought charming. "I shall hold Harry's vouchers for a time. Should such rumors get about, I shall immediately call them up." His face showed no emotion, but everyone in the room could see he meant every word. He watched Margaret's face harden into ugliness. A string of oaths burst forth from her mouth that made Angella gasp in shock beside him and jerk back.

"Take your milk-faced doxy then. It is not as though I can't find a more complacent husband."

The earl smiled. "But probably not one as deep in the pockets, eh. Be that as it may, I'll have the settlement papers drawn up. Harry, you will see my solicitor receives a list of your debts. Now," he said as he got to his feet, "I want you all out of here within the hour." With that, he assisted Angella to her feet, and, with his hand on her elbow, they started toward the door.

Margaret stopped him with "If she's as innocent as you say, how do you know her feelings for you are real instead of gratitude for taking her in? She knows nothing but you. How long before a younger, eligible parti turns her pretty little head?"

Her words pieced him like a sword. Was there truth to her accusation? He glanced toward Angella and away. She hadn't had much experience with men and what she had was not exactly positive. If she had other choices, would she still choose him? The thought was lowering. He'd have to think on it. For certain, he couldn't hurt her further.

Instead, the earl turned back. "Remember, I shall hold those debts to make sure you keep your word."

Behind them as they left the room, he heard Margaret mutter.

"You'll be sorry. You'll be sorry."

Was the woman speaking of him or of Angella? Neither thought was particularly appealing.

Angella was in her chamber when the earl saw off his former fiancée and her brothers. "I don't want you around them any longer," he told her. "You've borne quite enough from them. As soon as they leave, I'll come to you."

As much as Angella disliked the thought of Margaret's hatred, it was even more difficult to stay put in her room, not knowing what was happening below. The hour passed ever so slowly. The book she had been reading didn't hold her interest, and she placed it back on the shelf. Her hands moved over the soft calfskin covers of the other books.

The books were common enough in most establishments: Bunyon's *Pilgrim Progress, The Whole Duty of Man, Baker's Chronicles, The Tale of a Tub* and the

Complete Letter Writer. There were also several Gothic romances by the current rage Mrs. Radcliff, as well as a well-worn copy of the *The Vicar of Wakefield,* which Angella had been reading for the second time.

Sighing, she smoothed the skirt of her willow-green gown as she turned toward the window and looked out. At the moment she wished her windows overlooked the driveway. Then she could at least see whether or not Lady Margaret was, in truth, about ready to leave.

As much as she admired the earl's deft handling of the situation, she could not help but fear something would change, and Margaret would once more hold the reins of the situation—and the earl.

The hour passed, then two and still he did not come. Angella paced the room, unable to keep still. At the door, she heard the kitten scratching impatiently and hurried to let her in.

Cautiously, the little kitten poked her head in the room, meowing a question as she did so. As the kitten limped slowly into the room, Angella picked her up and cuddled her in her arms. "Poor baby. I'm so sorry you got hurt." A lump formed in her throat at the bandaged front leg. Mrs. Karry, knowing how the girl doted on the cat, had patched up the squirming animal and had Angella's maid inform her that the cat was all right when she brought up her chocolate that morning.

Rumors had spread rapidly and, by morning, the staff had a pretty good idea what had taken place the night before. Their sympathy was all for Angella. Mrs. Karry had clucked over her and the kitten as she once did over her own children, muttering darkly about ladies who were not ladies and gentlemen who were no gentlemen. The woman's vehemence brought a smile of understanding to Angella's lips. She felt like raging herself.

If only he would come. Fear nagged at her. She fair exploded with the waiting. Bowing her head, she prayed. Forced herself to pray even for a safe trip for Margaret and her brothers. As she prayed, a sweet calmness filled her heart as the verse which filled her mind during her brangle with Reverend Carter flowed into her heart.

Fear thou not; for I am with thee: be not dismayed; for I am thy God: I will strength thee; yea, I will help thee; yea, I will uphold thee with the right hand of my righteousness. Fear thou not; for I am with thee… Angella smiled. "Thank You, Jesus. Thank You."

When the earl came for her sometime later, she met him with a serene smile. "Spensor?"

He wasn't smiling. His whole demeanor confused her. He seemed somehow more distant now than ever. "Spensor? What is it? What's wrong? What has happened? She is gone, isn't she?"

The corners of the earl's lips turned up. "Oh, yes. She and her brothers are quite gone."

"So what about us?" asked Angella, searching the earl's face.

The earl took a deep breath. "I've been thinking. We've known each other for such a short time…"

Angella recalled Margaret's parting shot—*If she's as innocent as you say, how do you know her feelings for you are real instead of gratitude for taking her in?* A cold chill zipped down her spine. "True, but…"

He touched her face. "If what we have is real, it will grow stronger, not weaker, with time. You have so little experience of society. I want you to be sure."

"What does that mean?"

He took a deep breath. "For one thing, you cannot stay in my home without a chaperone or companion of some sort. Margaret was correct about that. It isn't right. I see that now. When I made that decision…"

Angella tried to quell the hurt inside, even as she realized the truth of what he said. "You really didn't care about a bedraggled, discarded, orphaned pastor's daughter."

A wry grin lit the earl's face. "You have the right of it."

"So what next?"

The earl paced the sitting room, before returning to where Angella awaited him. "In the spring, I propose to take you to London for the season."

"But, I don't want a season. I don't need a season." Angella tensed. "Do you fear I won't show well beside the haute ton?" She tried to keep the hurt from her tone.

Sitting down beside her, the earl took her cold hands in his. "No. No. But you are young and I want you to be sure, before you commit yourself for life. Will you be amenable to a season?"

"You really don't trust my feelings now?" Angella couldn't hide the hurt on her face.

"Will waiting change them?" The earl released one hand to tuck a strand of hair behind her ear.

What could she say? Would meeting other eligible young men change her feelings? She didn't think so. Her pained expression was enough. The earl nodded. His voice low. "You'll go, without tantrums or trying to run away?"

"I'll go." Her eyes widened as the thought crossed

her mind. "You won't leave me in London, will you?" Her hands grasped his.

"No. We'll give you the season your mother would want you to have."

Angella blinked tears. "I may not approve, but my mother would thank you," she said. "Before then? There is much time until spring."

The earl sucked in a breath. "I've already written to the Countess Winter about a visit. I was wrong in not allowing a chaperone, Angella."

"Do I really need a season?" Angella could not hide her trepidation. "All I've known is the village and a few celebrations at Lucashire here. I'm not ready…"

"The Earl of Alistair and his wife will add consequence to your season. Plus, Lady Winter can help show you how to get on in society." As though sensing her fear, he told her, "I watched how you comported yourself under the trial of Margaret's ire. You, not she, acted like the lady your mother taught you to be. You'll do fine, Angella."

He released her hands. "Now, I need to find you a companion." With that, he left her in the room, contemplating a totally different outcome to Margaret's visit than she expected.

Part of her wanted to go to London, another part wanted to run. She sighed. Too late for that now. Besides, she was rather curious about Lady Winter.

Chapter 9

The day after breaking his engagement, the earl called Trowbridge into his office. "I have something I wish you to do." He tented his fingers, wishing he hadn't made so many mistakes where Angella was concerned. He had fences to mend.

If nothing else, Margaret made him aware of his responsibilities. It was lowering to realize his own selfishness had led to the situation. "Angella needs a chaperone. Someone respectable and old enough to keep her presence here from gossip."

Trowbridge straightened. "Have anyone in mind?"

"I was wondering if, mayhap, I have some relative who needs a position. I do not know of any. You?"

The soldier shook his head. "However…" He hesitated.

"Out with it, man. I should have done this long past. If you have someone in mind, tell me."

"I do have a cousin, Alice. She lost her husband recently and hasn't the resources to support herself. In her late twenties. No children. He had a minor baron title, Lord Rathburn, and she was a lady from a good family."

Sponsor sat up. "Sounds just the thing for Angella. How soon can she be here?"

"I can have her here in a couple of days."

Sponsor nodded. "All right then. See if she'll come."

When Trowbridge introduced his cousin to Angella, they took to one another almost immediately. Alice added a quiet presence to meals and outings. Yet, she was allowed time alone to, as Angella told the earl, grieve for her husband and be treated as more friend than staff.

With that situation handled, the earl sent a letter to Alistair explaining the situation. Two weeks later, he handed Angella and Alice into a carriage, while he mounted a tall gelding, for a trip to visit Lord and Lady Alistair.

The earl sighed when he learned from Trowbridge, that Reverend Carter made much of their travel.

Once Angella had Alice to chaperone her, the earl did his best to keep their relationship friendly but not intimate. He didn't like the question in Angella's eyes whenever she looked at him. Didn't like the fire that seemed to have gone from her. He was thankful she seemed to accept their arrangement to be little more than guardian and ward.

Despite Sponsor's sometimes strange behavior toward her, Angella enjoyed the time they spent with

Alistair and Winter at their country home. She also enjoyed getting to know their rather rambunctious little boys. Winter made her feel at home and was more like a mother than an older sister. Lady Winter was not loathe to chide Spensor for not providing a chaperone immediately. She told them, "However, if Margaret will indeed keep her peace, we should be all right, especially since you are spending this time with us."

Angella and Winter enjoyed long rides on the well-manicured parks of the large estate, where Winter shared with Angella her own story of losing her father and of Alistair forcing her into a London season. Alice, who did not care for riding, usually asked to be excused from such outings.

"You didn't want a season, either?"

Winter smiled at her. "I was content with Renton Hall, my horse and my little dog. Or thought I was until Alistair showed up at my door thinking to make provisions for this poor girl with limitations. Instead, he found me and I read a peal over his head."

Angella had noticed, but said nothing, of Winter's somewhat misshapen hands and her slight limp. But once she got to know Winter, those things faded from her mind as though they didn't exist. She did not know how to ask but ventured shyly, "Did you ever wonder about, well, if he really cared for you?"

Lady Alistair turned intense blue eyes toward her until Angella grew uncomfortable and gripped the reins more tightly. "I see," she said, and Angella feared she saw too much indeed. "Yes, to your question. But it all came out right in the end."

Angella sighed. "I hope so. I truly hope so."

* * *

The earl strove to keep his growing feelings for Angella behind a mask of indifference. He tried to keep his feelings from Alistair, as well, but not so successfully. As they sat in the library with the women off visiting Alistair's brother and sister-in-law at Renton Hall, Alistair broached the subject. "Winter is quite taken with your ward."

"Angella can use friends."

"Winter was once my ward, as well, and I married her."

A muscle twitched in Spensor's cheek. Alistair obviously knew. No sense to pretend elsewise. "She has little experience with men. I want her to know her mind on this."

"Winter also had little experience. You might recall that bringing her to London almost got her killed." Spensor heard the pain in the man's voice even years later.

"I am no longer involved in the war effort like we were then."

"True. Still and all, be careful with her heart. London may not prove to be what you hope." For a moment, both men remained silent before Alistair made a suggestion. "Let her have her season without the complication of your feelings."

Later, after hearing his advice, Winter countered. "If her love is real, no one else will matter." She also cautioned, "But you are opening up yourself and her to great misunderstanding. This can lead to disaster." She clasped her hands.

Spensor wondered about her words and yet he settled for Alistair's advice. He cared enough for Angella to give her a season. The only problem was what to do about his own heart in the meantime.

As December stormed into January, the earl brought Angella and Alice back to Lucashire. He often talked about her London season. One evening as they sat by the fire, Angella continued the embroidery in her hands for a few moments as though gathering her thoughts. Finally, she spoke. "Lady Alistair, Winter, said they're opening Alistair House and would welcome us. But I… I'm still afraid of all that goes into a season."

She turned to Alice. "What about your season?"

Lady Rathburn smiled a sad smile. "I'm afraid mine was short. I found Rathburn almost right away—or we found each other. We married and left London. I never regretted that."

The earl cleared his throat. "Fear. I thought that might be a problem." He sat back, "I have already invited my aunt Helga, Lady Carrington, to visit us. She's popping off her daughter, Betsy, this season. I figured she could help you prepare, as well." The earl thought he'd handled that right well.

"I don't know." Angella remained uncertain. "Mayhap…"

"You met her daughter, Betsy, years ago. She told me of your kindness during my birthday celebration when the other young people made fun of her."

"Oh, yes, I remember your cousin. She was sweet." Angella smiled. "I'd like to get to know her better."

"Trust me, Angella. It will be all right. You and Betsy will be fast friends."

"You are kind to arrange the visit. I'll feel much better not going on alone." She sighed.

The earl cleared his throat. Angella's nearness was nearly his undoing. In truth, he did not want to take her to London, did not want her to meet other young men—gentlemen who might steal her heart. It was lowering to realize that the man who never concerned himself with his acceptability toward any woman was undone by one lovely young vicar's daughter.

As Alistair explained, though, Angella needed an opportunity to experience life outside her small village.

As she surveyed him, Angella's gaze held such tenderness. When she looked at him like that, he wanted to give her the moon. Instead, he must not think only of his own desires.

When not wrangling about the particulars of the London season, the earl and Angella spent time talking, discussing and arguing. They played games and deepened their understanding of one another. Most important, they began spending time each evening reading God's Word.

Starting with Matthew, they began to read through the New Testament. When a question arose, they discussed the passage. At first, the earl deferred to her to understand. But as he became more familiar with the Bible, he sometimes questioned her point of view. At first, it almost angered Angella. After all, she was a vicar's daughter and had been taught scripture since she was in leading strings. She kept her feelings inside, and slowly began to realize that Spensor's walk with God was deep and sincere. His understanding of scripture was beginning to surpass her own. At times, she was awed by his insight.

"Spensor, I never saw that passage in that way before." She shook her head. "I cannot wait for you to meet Edward."

During those times of contemplation, Angella knew God's love, but she also sensed the earl's care for her. Maybe a London season wouldn't be so bad—not if he was there along with his aunt, his cousin Betsy and Lady Winter.

Even though the earl no longer talked about a future together, he was a far different man from the cynical peer she first met on the road. He smiled more often these days—genuine smiles that reached his eyes.

Even with the visit to Lord and Lady Alistair, even with the presence of Alice with them constantly, the winter with Angella proved both restful and revitalizing for the earl. Not once did he miss the glitter and fast pace of the city, not once did he yearn for the late nights and shallowness of the beau monde.

Together, he and Angella rode, laughing as they raced along the hard-packed wood lawn paths. In the evenings after dinner, they often ended up in lively discussion such as he never envisioned having with other than his gentlemen friends. Alice seldom added much to the conversation, though on occasion she defended Angella's opinion on a matter—much to his chagrin.

Though Angella had the keeping of the manor, he was not loathe to share with her the problems he ran into during the day on the estate even as she shared with him. Though she offered good advice and suggestions, she deferred to his final decisions. Through it all, though he kept it to himself, his love for Angella grew, as well as the realization that Margaret would never have been a true helpmate to him. Over and over, he gave thanks for the wonderful gift he'd been given.

Those times each night reading God's Word were precious times, especially when they prayed for each other.

As the chill of winter eased, the earl told her, "Aunt Helga and Betsy will be here in a fortnight."

Angella paced the floor. "The closer the time comes, the more I wish I hadn't promised not to cause a problem over going to London for the season."

"There is nothing to worry about, Angella."

"Your aunt. What will she think of me? I have no polish and no desire to be paraded around London drawing rooms."

"Aunt Helga is not like that. She's a true lady and not all starched up like some ladies I can name—or won't name." Both knew he referred to Margaret. "You met my aunt before."

"But only as the vicar's daughter." She frowned. "I also talked to her when your father held a reception for Edward when he was commissioned as a missionary."

"You were kind to her daughter. She isn't likely to forget."

"What about Margaret?" Angella sucked in a breath before continuing. "Will she be in London?"

"I do not know." He lifted her chin. "She will not hurt you. I still hold her brother's debts—for now."

Angella sighed. "Is this really necessary?"

Taking her hand, the earl drew her to his side. "Actually, yes. Though, for the moment, Margaret is biding her time in the country, she will eventually return to

London. That we can count on. I want the ton to get to know you as you, before Margaret has her say."

"But the debts…?" Angella's eyes mirrored her uncertainty.

"For the time being they hold her in check, but I can't hold on to those vouchers forever. Trust me, Harry's debts are a heavy burden." He sighed.

"Spensor, I'm so sorry. I didn't realize. Surely then we need to economize."

"Nothing of the kind," he growled. "'Tis best we bring you out now, before I tear up those bothersome vouchers. Once they know they're free, Margaret, along with Harry, will return to London and to their old ways."

"She'll try to cause trouble."

He nodded. "I know Margaret…all too well," he added, his tone dry. He sensed Angella's reluctance. Again and again he tried to reassure her, though he was hard put not to keep her from recognizing his own hesitations.

After Spensor told her stories of his visits to Lady Carrington, Angella began to look forward to seeing Spensor's aunt and cousin. Maybe it wouldn't be the nightmare she envisioned with a starched-up socialite turning up her nose at Angella and her situation. In a better frame of mind, she worked with the housekeeper to ready the house for the arrival of Lady Carrington and Betsy.

But Lady Carrington did not arrive on the day specified. "They probably got delayed," the earl told Angella. However, his aunt and her daughter did not arrive the next day, either. On the third day, Angella witnessed the tightness in the earl's shoulders and the drawn appearance of his expression.

"I fear something is amiss," he said. "I think I'll ride out and see what has delayed them."

"And I'll pray." Angella stepped closer to him. "I know she's your favorite aunt and Betsy is your favorite cousin."

The earl squeezed her shoulder in gratitude. "I appreciate the prayers. Reminds me to do some praying of my own."

Before the long-legged gray stallion was brought around for him, a messenger arrived. Once the man had been sent on his way, Spensor stared at Angella, seeming almost afraid to open the note.

Angella led the way into the east parlor, where they both sat. With a deep sigh, Spensor opened the note and began to read. His shoulders relaxed and when he looked up, a slight smile sat on his lips.

Wrapping an arm around Angella's shoulders, he told her. "They are both all right. A horse spooked during one of Betsy's rides. Aunt Helga says Betsy ended up with a badly sprained arm. She is well enough, but Aunt Helga does not want to chance traveling now with Betsy."

The earl's gaze traced her lips. Angella's heart pounded as he drew close. Abruptly, he pulled back and removed his arm. "I'm sorry." Getting to his feet, he left the room.

Angella did not know whether to rage or cry. She did both. If Spensor was so loathe to be close to her here in his own home, what would he be like in London? Angella bowed her head and prayed.

* * *

They headed to London before the season even opened properly. Angella was glad for the presence of Alice in the carriage on the long, exhausting trip. For the most part, Spensor rode his magnificent chestnut gelding alongside their carriage. A couple of times, when the weather turned cold and windy, Spensor rode in the carriage with them. During those times he pointed out places of interest as they drove by. Still and all, his presence squeezed the space available and even Alice later mentioned the tension between the two of them when in close proximity.

Once they began to prepare for the trip, Angella felt the earl withdraw from her. Oh, he was unfailingly polite and all kindness itself, but he seemed to keep himself under tight control. It was a puzzle. All Angella knew was that she was relieved when they arrived at their destination.

Alistair and Winter had already taken up residence in Alistair House. "Oh, look!" Angella pointed toward the three-story structure with its tall round tower facing the street. "This is where we're staying?" Her gaze took in the dwelling as the driver pulled up the horses. The stone of the tower had been left rough, giving it character. The stonework was neatly pointed in red mortar. The rest of the building was of red-painted wood, with brick-red shutters on the tall windows.

The earl escorted Angella to the door, with Alice following. As the butler opened the door and ushered them inside, Lady Alistair greeted her and Alice. As soon as he greeted his hostess, Spensor went to find Alistair.

Lady Alistair led Angella and Alice through the lobby with its tiled floor polished until she could see her reflection. The spacious hall had a window seat, as did the arched library. At the far end, an elegant staircase with carved banister and gilt newels flowed upward to the chambers on the next floor.

The parlor, with its cherry paneling, had a redbrick fireplace, tiled hearth and facings along with a hardwood mantel. The gracious dining room with its long Chippendale furnishings was trimmed in maple.

"It's magnificent." Angella ran her slender fingers over the polished face of the built-in buffet with all its ornamented drawers holding the silver, and the shelves which held the Alistair crested china. The floor in the dining room and the library was a mosaic of oak, maple and mahogany.

Alice asked to be shown to Angella's room, and Winter summoned a maid for that purpose. "I'll just start unpacking your things, Miss Denning."

Angella noted her drawn expression and touched her shoulder. "Then you rest a bit before dinner."

Alice smiled. "Thank you. I'll do that."

After Alice's departure, Winter took Angella through the up-to-snuff kitchens, wainscoted and trimmed in white pine. The staff bustled about them with a contented air.

"Fixin' yer favorite puddin' fer dinner, Your Ladyship," said the portly cook with apple cheeks.

Angella's admiration for Lady Alistair grew as she spoke personally and knowledgeably with the servants. "They think very highly of you, Winter," she whispered. "You are wonderful to them."

Finally, she followed the countess up the wide staircase to the bedchambers. She was astonished at the large armoire and the necessary off her rooms. "Slap dash up to the mark." She grinned as Lady Alistair groaned at her use of the cant phrase.

"Truly, the room is beautiful." She gazed about at the light graceful furniture, the blue velvet curtains and bed hangings. She smoothed the counterpane on the bed. "It looks new."

"I had it redone especially for you. I'm glad you like it." Winter spread her arms. "I wanted you to be comfortable here. A London season is exhausting at best, and I want you to have some privacy and a place to rest."

Angella sat on the settee by the hearth. "I fear I am not ready to be flaunted in London drawing rooms. What do I have to flaunt? I'm the daughter of a poor vicar."

"With a starched-up grandfather, so I hear."

"True, but he wants nothing to do with either my brother or me." The knowledge still stung.

"Maybe not, but letting the ton know of the connection cannot hurt…."

"I wish the Earl of Lucashire was not so insistent on my having a season." Her clenched fists revealed her nervousness.

Winter sat beside her. Her tone was quiet. "You will please him by making the most of this opportunity. With your portion…"

Angella's head snapped up. "I have no portion."

Winter bit her lip and turned away. "I thought you knew."

Reaching for Winter's arm, Angella drew her attention. "Knew what?"

"Lucashire settled a portion on you."

Finally Angella understood. She whispered, "He hopes some peer with pockets to let will ask for my hand. But I thought…" She turned away. Spensor wanted to rid himself of her, did he? Then she would take in the season, but never, never would she allow herself to be sold to the highest bidder. Never! Confused, Angella's love for the stubborn man warred with her fury.

Chapter 10

Less than a week later, the earl, who seemed to have no notion of Angella's feelings, reintroduced her to his aunt, Lady Carrington, a woman of ample proportions and a pleasant if not beautiful face. Angella curtsied, but Lady Carrington would have none of that. She surprised Angella with a hug. "Call me Aunt Helga, like Spensor here."

Angella blushed, not at all sure what to do. The earl shrugged. "Better do as she requests, Angella. She's been bossing me around since I was in leading strings."

Angella couldn't help but laugh at his expression of half horror and half admiration. "Thank you...Aunt Helga."

Spensor also reintroduced her to Betsy. The younger woman, of an age with Angella, had little to recommend her, being tall and thin with a rather plain face. What

Angella remembered most was her merry brown eyes, which were a definite asset, and her gorgeous thick hair.

Betsy also hugged her. "I'm so glad Spensor brought you to London, too. I won't feel quite so alone in this venture."

Angella's fears evaporated and she smiled in relief. "I'm glad you're here, too. I was dreading the season. How is your arm? I am sorry you injured yourself."

Betsy moved her arm. "Still a little stiff and sore, but much better."

In the two days before Lady Carrington and Betsy's arrival, Winter had lost no time in taking Angella to the dressmakers, shoemaker and a dozen other establishments in order to acquire all the accoutrements deemed necessary for the season.

"This is too much!" Angella had exclaimed. "Surely I won't require all of this."

"That is what I thought," Winter told her. "I was horrified at the number of gowns and other fripperies purchased for me." She sighed. "You'll find you'll need this and more. I'm afraid this is only the beginning. We will have more shopping to do once Betsy arrives." Angella gulped.

Lady Alistair also took her to afternoon tea and encouraged Spensor to ride with her in the park. "Afraid, my dear, it is all about being seen." She rolled her eyes until Angella laughed. Somehow Winter made it all less frightening.

At a quiet garden party, Angella overheard a couple of older ladies chatting over their tea and sweets. "She's comely enough. The earl is doing well by her."

A lady in deep fuchsia nodded. "Yes, with the portion he's settled on her, some dandy should come up to scratch. Good family on her mother's side."

A third fanned her face. "Hear Lady Carrington is bringing out her daughter with Miss Denning."

"So I hear," the second woman commented. "Not quite the thing. Her mother was top-drawer in her prime. Sad the daughter is more of an antidote."

"And with so little portion."

Angella started toward the women, angry and ready to speak her mind. Winter grabbed her arm. "It will do her no good and you harm, Angella. Let it go."

Now that Betsy had arrived, Angella found her to be a quiet but kind young woman, and the remarks she'd heard seemed even more unfair and cruel.

Together with Lady Winter, Betsy and Lady Carrington, Angella spent the next couple of weeks in an endless round of shopping the posh shops on Bond Street and visiting those dressmakers catering to the whims of the ton. The women purchased a horrendous number of gowns, slippers and other fripperies the earl insisted she and Betsy required in order to be properly presented. Winter was right. The shopping they did before Betsy's arrival had been just the beginning.

At the earl's command, Angella forced herself to forget the prodigious cost of her purchases, especially after the earl assured her he was not spending money he did not have, nor was he taking what should have been spent on his estate.

The whole exercise exhausted her, and she was glad they had arrived in London before the season opened. But shopping was only part of what awaited her. One morning Winter introduced the girls to their new dancing master. The man was tall, thin and dressed in the first stare of fashion. His expression was haughty, as though he lowered himself to teach two unfledged chits the finer steps in the dances currently all the rage.

Betsy stifled a giggle and gained a glare. Angella rolled her eyes as the man positively pranced about the room. Nonetheless, his lessons did make Angella less concerned with that aspect of the balls, routs and other events that would require her to dance. The country dances in Little Cambrage were rather informal events, and Angella later told Betsy, "At least now I'll know how to go on properly. Mayhap I won't tread upon my partners' toes."

She found Betsy of like mind about the lessons and the shopping. The two quickly became bosom bows and often shared a private coz in the afternoons—the few afternoons they had to themselves.

One afternoon as they sat enjoying tea, Betsy confided, "I know I'm no beauty, but Mother insists I have the bronze of a town season." Squeezing Angella's hand, she added as color flushed her pale cheeks, "I'm glad you're being presented, too, though it isn't quite the same. As the ward of Lucashire, you already are accorded more consequence than his lowly cousin." She smiled as if to take the sting from her comment.

"Mayhap, Betsy, but I'm hardly the sort the ton expected the earl to bring to London. I've overheard some rather pointed remarks on that score."

"Mayhap we should run away," suggested Betsy. "At least, me. I know I have little to recommend me but the family name and a small, but respectable portion." Her eyes clouded. "But I don't want to be foisted off on some fortune hunter. I want to have the sort of relationship my mother and father had, the sort of relationship Lord and

Lady Winter have. I see how they look at each other." She put her hands against her red cheeks. "Is that too much to ask for?"

Angella hugged the girl. "No, it isn't. God can do anything, Betsy. Trust Him and don't lose hope." Her words sounded hollow to her own ears, especially since the more she got involved in preparations for the season, the more Spensor absented himself from her life. She scarcely saw him anymore. All the preparations, clothes and lessons on behavior and manners seemed empty without his presence. "Lord," she begged at night. "Please take this love from my heart." But she felt the Lord was telling her to just love him. And wait.

Angella went to sleep wondering how to accomplish that, when the earl was seldom around. When he was present, he treated her with the affection of an older brother. Did he realize how much that hurt? Up until meeting the countess and getting more acquainted with Betsy and her mother, she envisioned all members of the ton (almost all, she thought, thinking of Spensor) as frivolous, shallow and selfish as Margaret and her brothers.

Had she not read of the fabulous parties, the disregard for the common man in the streets, the plight of the climbing boys and the homeless? Had she not scorned the prince regent for his excesses in entertainment and in his continual expensive improvements on Carlton House, as well as for his behavior with a succession of mistresses?

Lady Carrington, though, did something about the problems and it was not but two weeks after Aunt Helga's arrival in London that Angella found herself distributing food to the orphans in the orphan homes and clothes to those in workhouses. Lady Carrington did not just mouth platitudes of sorrow over the bleak situation in the streets, she and Betsy did their utmost to address the needs. On occasion, Lady Alistair, when she could get away from her obligations and the two children, joined them.

Once Spensor realized what they were about, he insisted either he or Lord Alistair offer them support and protection on the sordid, dangerous backstreets where his aunt insisted on going. "Half her friends dread seeing her on their doorstep," he teased. "They know she'll have them out of one thing or another before she leaves." He winked. "She is a past master at the guilt factor."

For all his jesting, Angella could see he was proud of his aunt. "I've not always admired her work," he admitted to Angella, "but I always admired her spunk. She, at least, is no hypocrite." His face darkened and Angella caught a glimpse of the cynical man he used to be.

One afternoon, Lucashire took her arm as they ambled down the flagstone path in the newly awakening flower garden. "I fear you'll find many who'll toad eat to your face, then repeat vicious lies behind your back." Pausing, he faced her, indecision on his face. "Angella, mayhap I should not have brought you to London after all. You are so innocent and inexperienced. I don't want you hurt. You've suffered enough because of the pompous Reverend Carter, not to mention Margaret and her brothers." His expression was pensive.

"Thank you for your concern, Spensor, but it doesn't signify. The reason still exists for my having a season now." She managed a half smile. "At least I'll have you and Winter, Betsy and your dear aunt beside me. It'll be all right." She sighed. "I just wish…"

"What? What do you wish?"

Angella turned from him, her voice low. "That you were not gone so often. I know about the portion you settled on me."

The silence forced her to glance up to find the earl frowning down at her. "I see."

"I won't be sold off like one of your prized blood cattle."

Puzzlement crossed his face. "Of course not. Why would you think such a thing?" He held her arm more tightly. She pulled away.

"You could have simply said you wanted to get me off your hands. No, instead you go to this elaborate, and expensive, ruse to get me… Where?"

"No. You don't understand, Angella. It isn't like that at all."

She wanted to stamp her foot and march off. Instead, tears started in her eyes. A yawn hit her unprepared.

Concern showed in his eyes. "You've been doing too much, Angella. What with running about doing good works with Aunt Helga, all that shopping and fitting. The season is exhausting enough without going into it fatigued." He saw hesitation on her face.

"You *are* dreading it, aren't you?"

Reluctantly, Angella nodded. "I am. I'm a bit run-down. And you are always any place but here."

He touched her face. "I'm sorry. But you did practically shame me into doing my duty in the chambers."

"Truly, you are getting involved?" Mayhap she'd had some positive influence.

"I am. Politics takes time, my dear."

She sensed he held something back, but his apology did much to soothe her wounded heart.

"I shall explain to Aunt Helga that you've had enough for now. No more running here and there. For a few days at least, we shall spend our days quietly."

Angella threw her arms about his neck. "Thank you. I'd like that above anything."

Betsy came on them in that moment. Later, she quizzed Angella. "I think I'm beginning to understand."

Angella bit her lip. "What?"

"You and Spensor. You care for him."

"He is my guardian after all."

"Um, that explains the look in his eyes. He cares for you, too."

"Sure. That's why he stays away so much of the time." She realized she sounded petty. "I mean…"

Betsy smiled. "No need to explain. I understand."

"I don't."

"You do care for him?"

Angella nodded. "I know I'm not some grand personage, but…I thought…"

"He cares, as well. But he's giving you a season." Betsy giggled. "He's taking the position of your parents…or your brother. He has to play the guardian, not the jealous suitor—don't you see?"

Could that be true? It was something to consider— especially since Betsy began to make it a point to find ways to throw them together. If only Edward would come home, things would be a whole lot less complicated.

In her few quiet moments, she prayed for Edward's safety and wondered where he was. Then, as the season got into full swing, Angella had little time to think of Edward or his inevitable visit. There was the ball at Lady Denton's dark, Gothic home, and the musical at the home of a duke. She was excited to spend an evening at the theater and stroll with the earl in the company of Betsy, her mother and Lord and Lady Alistair down the Grand Walk of Vauxhall Gardens. She loved listening to organist Mr. James Hook. Alistair told them Hook had been featured at the gardens since 1774.

At the events for young ladies being "popped off" during the season, she met other young women as unsure as she was herself. She found herself feeling older than some who were terrified they'd end up with some horrible, old, ugly or mean husband that satisfied their parents' idea of a good match—someone with money and a title. At least she did not think she need worry about that, though Spensor seemed less than pleased when some eligible men paid her fulsome compliments and seemed eager to gain her favor.

Baron Farnsworth was a fop of a man who spent most of the time talking about himself. He had little knowledge of anything outside his own interests. The older Viscount of Endenon hung on to her arm whenever he got close enough, making it difficult for her to evade him. Betsy, at times, came to her rescue. Others whom she met proved to be forgettable, especially when she compared them to Spensor.

A fortnight later, Angella tore open a letter handed her by the majordomo, Davis, a permanent fixture of Alistair House. Angella stilled a giggle at the starched manner of the butler.

As the butler marched out the door, Spensor entered the room. "A letter? What is it, another invitation to some boring theatrical or rout?" He frowned. "From another silly coxcomb, I presume."

The letter forgotten, Angella's expression softened

and she touched his cheek. "You have no call to be jealous, Spensor." Her gaze narrowed. "Those coxcombs, as you call them, would not be trying to sit in my pocket if you had not decided to make known you are providing a substantial portion when I marry."

The earl sucked in a breath. "Farnsworth has been most attentive."

"Farnsworth is a twaddling idiot. As you well know."

"The Viscount of Endenon danced three dances with you at the last rout. Not seemly for an unfledged chit and quite beyond the pale."

"I fear he gave me little chance to say no." Angella shook her head. "His stays creaked the entire time. He breathed so hard, I thought he was going to have an attack."

"He is considered a good catch." The earl wouldn't let it go. "The Marquis of Avendan has been trying to sit in your pocket, as well."

"He is too encroaching by half." Angella gritted her teeth. The others who paid her attention, she could shrug off. The marquis, however, seemed particularly possessive.

She had met him the night she attended a ball at Chesterfield House. The white marble grand staircase was magnificent with the colorful and bejeweled ladies walking up the stairs beside their fashionable escorts. Angella had actually looked forward to the evening and hoped to tour some of the rooms.

Instead, the Marquis of Avendan approached and asked for a dance. Without another thought, Angella nodded and held out her hand. Unfortunately, the marquis drew her close and held her more tightly than manners dictated. Though she tried to move away, he acted as though he had no notion she was uncomfortable. Even after that dance, she found it difficult to escape his determination to stay near. Since that night, she'd been hard-pressed to discourage his interest. His presence quite spoiled several outings for her.

But Spensor wouldn't listen to her protestations of disinterest. He'd been like this since they came to London. All she wanted to do was to have him tell her he still cared. Instead, he pushed her into meeting one eligible parti after another, then got angry when she treated the gentlemen with little more than gentle kindness or, in the marquis's case, sought to avoid him at all cost.

She was glad for the support of Winter and glad Spensor had agreed to stay in London with Lady Alistair, her husband and their two young children.

Remembering the letter she held in her hand, Angella turned over the missive to read the address. Suddenly she tensed. "Spensor, look. It's from Edward, my brother. He must have finally gotten my letter about..." She gulped. "Mother and Father." The earl's frown eased and he drew Angella close.

For a moment, she clung to him before he drew her toward the long brocade-covered sofa in the morning room. Smoothing down the long spring-green velvet skirt of her gown, she sat next to Spensor.

Opening the envelope addressed in an unfamiliar hand to her and the earl, she found a smaller envelope addressed to Miss Angella Denning, Little Cambrage. She wondered who had sent the letter on. Not that it mattered as long as she received it. Her hands shaking with anticipation, Angella unfolded the page and scanned it, then read through it more slowly. A radiant smile lit her face.

Hugging the earl, she cried, "He received my letter, Spensor! Edward is coming home!"

The earl took the letter from her trembling fingers. "Yes, but we have no idea when. But at least when he wrote this, he had booked passage on a ship to England.

"Besides," the earl continued, "I'm sure he'll wish to return to Little Cambrage first, since he has no notion you are here in London." The earl checked the envelopes. "He cannot know our direction here in London at Alistair House."

Angella bit her lip in excitement. "Oh, Spensor, I can't wait to see him!" Her smile of excitement dimmed. "What if he wants to take me away? He is my guardian after all."

"What would disturb you—" the earl ran a gentle finger against her cheek before continuing "—leaving all this…or me?"

Angella sensed pain in her erstwhile guardian.

The earl couldn't help but wonder if bringing her to London had been a mistake. She seemed to like the attention, the teas, parties, balls and routs. All he wanted was to make sure Angella loved him for himself alone. So why did she have to enjoy the parties and routs so much? Did she hold feelings for those who flocked around her? She said no, but he struggled to keep jealousy at bay. The best he could manage was to absent himself on a regular basis.

Angella scrunched up her face. "Spensor? What's wrong?" She leaned against him, but he pulled back as though burned. Hurt flashed on her face.

"Nothing's wrong," he growled. Again, he wished for those days when he had her all to himself. He was surprised Alice was not with Angella. She was usually nearby.

When it wasn't Alice, it was Betsy, who'd figured out he had feelings for Angella. Still and all, Betsy's attempts to push them together made for awkward moments, though he couldn't fault his cousin. Betsy saw through his indifference to his heart and wanted only what was best for him. The minx was not loathe to meddle. He could only hope after the season ended, Angella would choose him.

Suddenly Angella straightened, drawing his attention back to the present. "Oh, no… Reverend Carter! Edward will go straight to the vicarage."

"You're right. I thought the bounder would be long gone by now. I half wish I hadn't given him the choice to stay until he found another living. I wonder how hard he's been looking." The earl frowned, then said, "Mayhap I'd better write my manager to be on the lookout for your brother. I fear Reverend Carter has little love for either of us."

Some of the happiness faded from Angella's eyes. "That so-called minister has the whole village under his thumb." She let out a long sigh. "The lies he tells them about us. How can such a man call himself a man of God?"

"Unfortunately, our clergy are not all called of God, not when the church is the repository of the younger sons of English peers." The earl's hold on Angella tightened. "I've waited far too long. Time I give him an ultimatum."

"I'm glad." She hid her face against his shoulder

and he had little incentive to pull away. "He was so awful. First him, then Margaret and her brothers..." Angella sighed.

It seemed so long ago now since he sent away Lady Margaret and her brothers. They had not seen them since, much to his relief. If only they stayed away.

Chapter 11

Angella, looking ethereal, floated down the staircase in a gown that flattered her petite figure.

The white silk skirt and sleeves shimmered with pearls. The heart-shaped neckline dipped modestly to the white velvet bodice. The gently puffed sleeves shirred to the elbow, ending with white velvet bows. The silvery sash about her waist widened in the back into a mini train. The diamond tiara glittering in her hair matched the diamonds in her ears, around her neck and on her delicate wrist.

The earl, holding her arm, smiled down at her in admiration. "Top drawer. Quite up to snuff."

They reached the ballroom and she grinned at him mischievously as she looked him up and down. "Up to snuff yourself." Though she teased, there was no denying her heart beat faster at the sight of Spensor in his deep blue formal jacket, silver embroidered waistcoat and formal breeches.

Returning her grin, he touched the tip of her nose. "Better hope so, considering Prince Regent himself promised to make an appearance this evening. Actually, Prinny said he might make this the first stop of his evening's schedule. That should put you in high gig."

"Put me in a proper spin, more like," said Angella, rolling her eyes. A moment later she was distracted as the housekeeper hurried up to her, all aflutter.

"The cake is all to pieces, and the extra help hasn't arrived and…" The woman all but moaned. "Why did Her Ladyship have to leave now?"

Angella wished, too, that Alistair and Winter were present for the ball given in her honor. Unfortunately, Alistair's brother's wife's child was coming earlier than expected and there was concern for her welfare. Winter wanted to be with her sister-in-law and friend, Mary. Winter told stories to Angella that made her jaw drop. How brave Winter had been during her season to confront spies and more. Her sister-in-law had been undercover then as Winter's abigail. There were still aspects of what went on during that time that could not be revealed—especially with the war still lingering on. Angella said a quick prayer for the safety of Mary and her baby.

Then, taking the housekeeper's arm, Angella threw the earl a look of apology. She hated to leave him when they seemed in charity with one another. "Come. Let's see what we can do about these problems," she soothed the woman.

By the time Angella had calmed the housekeeper, suggested cutting the cake and offering it on separate plates, Davis, the majordomo, announced in his deep tones, "Lady Carrington and Lady Elizabeth." Angella hugged them with relief.

"Thank you both for getting back early," said Angella. "I know your work at the mission is important, but I am so glad you are back."

"Lady Alistair is still gone?" Betsy glanced about.

Angella, took her arm. "It's been almost a week now. I know they hoped to be back, but…"

"I am so sorry." Lady Carrington gave her a quick hug. "But, my dear, you'll be fine. Truly, you've done well. The decorations are all finished. We'll help as needed. Now, I do not want you to concern yourself further."

Angella's cheeks reddened. "Thank you, but Aunt Helga, I have another desperate problem. The extra help His Lordship hired hasn't arrived and the housekeeper is all in pieces as to how to deal with the crush without adequate staff."

Lady Carrington patted her arm. "Now, don't get in a taking, dear. I'll see to it. Don't worry, we'll soon have all the help we need."

True to her word, within the hour the Alistair House buzzed with the influx of staff, and the housekeeper hurried about, happily instructing each of his or her place for the evening.

"I don't know what I'd do without you, Aunt Helga." Angella gave her a hug. "Thank you."

Coming into the room, the earl strode to her side. "Do I warrant one of those?"

As she pretended to consider, the earl grinned. Angella wished he truly cared. "Spensor, we have an audience."

His smile wavered. "One of your flirts, no doubt." He started to turn away. Angella felt her heart sink and her anger rise. *Frustrating man!*

The doorbell rang. "Come on, you two." Lady Carrington straightened. "Time to look sharp."

Before they took their places in line, Betsy whispered to Angella. "If Avendan bothers you tonight, stand by me. Together we'll discourage him. All right?"

Angella hugged her, glad she'd confided in the younger woman. "Thanks. That helps."

Lady Carrington took her place on the other side of Angella, with her daughter on the far side of the reception line.

Angella's insides churned and she sucked in a deep breath to steady her nerves. Leaning over, Spensor whispered. "No matter what, Angella, remember…I am proud to be here with you."

His words warmed something inside her. As Angella flashed him a grateful smile, Betsy asked, "Is it true, His Royal Highness is attending this evening's affair?"

The earl laughed. "So he said, Betsy."

The girl's face whitened. "Oh, dear. I think I shall faint dead away when he takes my hand. He's so charming, but I never know quite what to say to royalty."

There was no more time for chatter as the guests began to arrive. They quickly filled the ballroom Angella, Betsy and the servants had meticulously decorated with flowers and silver, blue and red streamers. Before long, Angella's fingers throbbed from shaking endless hands, and her smile seemed permanently locked in place on her aching face.

The cream of London's society passed down the line.

There was the Duke of York, Lord Alvanley, the Marquess of Hertford, Earl of Bradford.

There were political figures such as Lord Addington. Angella forced herself to respond to the panicky little man. She was much more effusive in welcoming Wilberforce. "Thank you," she told him, "for all you're doing to stop the inhumane practice of slavery."

The pale man's hand trembled in hers. "Thank you, m'lady. I understand you are the one to thank for Lucashire taking up my cause in chambers."

"She and Alistair," Spensor acknowledged. With a nod, the great man passed down the line with a word to Lady Carrington, whom he seemed to know quite well. Since Wilberforce was often ill, Angella was gratified by his presence.

Behind him was the Marquis of Avendan. His palms were damp and Angella had the desire to wipe her own on her gown. He held her hand so long, she tugged it away, flushing at the possessive look in his eyes.

The earl whispered, "Are you all right?"

Angella shrugged and quickly, too quickly, turned to the next person in line, a giggly young thing in a gossamer gown the color of amethyst that set off her eyes. Angella recalled meeting her a few times at different events. The girl glanced toward the marquis, then blushed with embarrassment when he all but ignored her. Moments later the line stalled. Glancing down the queue, Angella sighed.

But Lady Carrington kept the line moving along. Though they waited several minutes after all the other guests had been greeted, the prince regent did not arrive.

"One never knows about him," said the earl, finally

breaking line. Taking Angella's arm, he whispered, "I'm sure he means no disrespect to you, Angella. Probably stuck somewhere else."

Angella stifled a giggle. "I'm not going into decline over it, Spensor. To own the truth, I'm relieved."

He squeezed her hand. "That a girl."

He swung around as Davis's tone deepened even further and mingled with awe as he announced the royal arrival. With the announcement, the earl stepped back in line, pulling Angella into line as Lady Carrington did her daughter. Graciously, the earl welcomed the regent and introduced Angella. "My ward, Angella Denning."

Surveying her until she blushed, the regent bent to kiss Angella's hand, holding it much longer than politeness dictated. His stays, meant to hold in his rotund middle, squeaked ominously, but Angella pretended not to notice.

At her blush, he chuckled. "Now, my dear, always good to make the man a trifle jealous," he said, assuming his marked attentions, not his stays caused the flush in her cheeks. "Keeps him in line, you know."

Angella flushed, wishing what the regent said was actually true—that Spensor cared about her.

"Angella needs not such tactics, Your Highness."

Hearing the mild reproof, Angella glanced at him, then back at the prince, hoping the regent would not take offense. The next king merely laughed and moved on. He did, however, make a point to seek her out later, before he took his leave.

"Lovely evening, my dear. I'll have to see you at Carlton House soon."

To own the truth, Angella, busy with her duties, found the evening more relaxing once he had gone. She and the earl mingled with their guests. With the volatile mixture of political sentiments present, they were careful to keep their more explosive guests from one another. Though several of the women eyed her speculatively, she sensed no overt animosity. It was lowering to realize they saw in her no threat.

When the earl bowed and took her hand for the opening dance, Angella blushed and tried to keep her feelings from showing in her expression. Dancing with Spensor was a dream come true, and she floated more than danced. The joy of that dance set the tone for the evening. Though she hoped for more, while the earl danced with other women in attendance, he never again sought her hand.

Determined not to let him dampen her enjoyment of her ball, Angella plastered on a smile and danced with the gentlemen who asked. As she whirled around the floor on the arms of one or another of the gentlemen, she was gratified to see that Betsy had her share of partners, as well. For all that, she did her best to avoid the Marquis of Avendan, though she often found his gaze upon her.

When she least expected it, the marquis took her arm. She jerked back in surprise.

A serious expression sat on his lips. "You have been avoiding me, my dear. Shall we?" He half bowed and indicated the dance floor.

What she wanted to do was turn her back. But he'd done nothing overtly to suffer a cut. Angella glanced around, hoping to see the earl, Betsy or Lady Carrington, but everyone was otherwise engaged.

"Surely the vicar's daughter cannot think she's above my touch."

"Hardly." His sarcasm stiffened her resolve. What could the man do in the sad crush? There were people everywhere. He surely could not propose marriage in the middle of a packed ballroom or act like the vicar. Surely she was safe here. With some trepidation, Angella put her hand in the marquis's. The moment he closed his hand over hers and led her onto the floor, Angella realized she'd made the wrong choice, though she had no idea how she could have refused him without causing a stir. He was a marquis after all.

He pulled her closer than she preferred and she was glad when they parted in the dance. His gaze held hers and when he did hold her arm, his grip was firm. She started when he leaned close and whispered for her ears alone, "I mean to have you as my wife, Angella. Remember that."

"What?" she stammered.

He held her tightly when she tried to pull away. "You can't get away from me, you know."

"I hardly know you, sir. Besides, what would a man of your stature want with a vicar's daughter?"

"There would be no objection to a vicar's daughter with a nice settlement."

"So that's all you're after," she spat. "There are plenty of women with 'nice settlements,' as you so elegantly put it. Many have a bigger share than do I, so why don't you pursue one of them?"

"My dear," he practically purred, "none have such a pretty face and figure. And your mother's family is up to snuff. Your grandfather has a title and deep pockets. You are quite acceptable as the wife of a marquis."

"You flatter yourself. If you think I will inherit anything from my grandfather, you are mistaken. He disowned his own daughter, and I have no illusions that he will change his will in my favor and leave me so much as a farthing. And I will thank you to remember that I am under the protection of an earl. I do not have to marry for a title—or any other reason. I'd rather be an impoverished spinster."

The marquis laughed. "By the looks of your gowns and fripperies, I would say that you enjoy having money too much to settle for being impoverished. And so do I. There's no law against marrying for money. Now, let us stop fencing. I think your earl will favor my suit. You wait and see."

When the set ended, she pulled away and hurried to find the earl. He didn't seem to be any place. Instead, she rushed to Lady Carrington's side. The marquis followed. In fact, every time she turned around, he was watching her, a look of ownership on his face.

She managed to forestall another turn on the floor in his arms, but wasn't able to keep him from escorting her down to supper, where he was most solicitous of her every want. She felt trapped by the man's attentions. She overheard comments that made her ill. "Look there, she has the marquis in her pocket."

"Wonder how long before he declares himself."

"And she only a vicar's daughter."

"But she has a goodly portion."

"There is that. Here tell, the marquis could use the portion."

Angella never knew how she managed to get through the ordeal without throwing her plate at the marquis. She saw her chance when an elderly peer greeted the marquis. With a nod, Angella graciously got to her feet. "I will leave you two to talk. I need to take a break."

With that, she hurried from the room and headed across the ballroom toward the terrace. All she wanted to do was get away from the false smiles and snide comments, get away from the marquis. Gentlemen requesting her hand for the dance seemed to be in short supply just when she hoped someone would rescue her.

Hearing a deep voice, she turned, fearing the marquis had come after her. Instead, she plowed headlong into the earl. "Whoa!" He gripped her upper arms to keep her from falling.

"Oh, Spensor, I am so glad to find you."

"Oh, really. What, you lose your precious marquis?"

"What? No, please. Listen. You must help me." She stared into the face of a stranger. Gone the gentle man who said he cared. This man was furious—and at her.

"I saw the two of you at supper. You certainly have his attentions. I'm sure you'll be delighted to know he asked for your hand. I said no, but I suppose I was wrong and you favor his suit."

"No. No! Spensor, please allow me to explain." He didn't let her finish.

"You women are all alike. You are not so different from Margaret after all. Out for the main chance. He has a better title and extensive lands, though you'll discover soon enough he doesn't have deeper pockets." He gave her a little shake. "I wish you well, Angella. Truly, I do…" Did she hear a catch in his voice?

Before she could say or do else, he released her so quickly she put a hand on the wall to keep her balance as she watched the earl stride down the hall and out of her sight.

"Oh, Lord. Please help me. Help Spensor realize the truth. Don't let him say yes to that odious man's suit."

Suddenly the excitement of the evening and the whole season disappeared. Without the earl's goodwill, Angella wanted nothing to do with any of it. She never cared for it overmuch anyway.

How could she return to the ballroom now? How could she put on a smile as though everything was all right? Without the earl's regard, nothing would ever again be all right. Exhaustion hit, deep-down exhaustion. Her legs felt heavy and she stepped out onto the terrace. All she wanted to do was escape to her room, but this evening was her ball, she had to go back. But first she would take a moment to pray.

Bowing her head, she let out a deep sigh. With a prayer, she sucked in a breath of fresh air, straightened her shoulders and turned. She would make her mother proud. Then, somehow, she would find the earl and force him to listen.

"Well, if it isn't my devoted dinner companion." Angella froze as she faced the marquis.

"It seems your guardian is finally ready to give his approval to our nuptials. As I said he would."

Angella forced a smile. "I fear he misunderstands the situation. You have not asked for my hand."

"My lady—" sarcasm laced his words "—will you do me the honor of becoming my wife?"

Angella's gaze narrowed. "No. I fear we will not suit. So I will tell my guardian."

"I see. The lowly vicar's daughter thinks she is someone because she has the approval of Alistair and Lucashire." He gripped her arm none too gently.

Angella gulped. "It does not signify. I will not marry you. Please let go of my arm. People are looking at us."

A slow smile played on the marquis's lips. "They

will only think we're having a lovers' quarrel. I'm sure you've heard the tittle-tattle tonight. It's all but assumed the announcement is forthcoming. You did not seem averse to my suit at dinner tonight. Everyone could see that."

"I was only being polite. I certainly did not encourage your attentions."

"Nonetheless, your so-called guardian has given his consent to our match, my dear. Now, are you ready to be sensible? We'll announce the news of our engagement tonight. What better time than your own ball?"

Swinging about, Angella ran toward the ballroom, praying for help as she felt the marquis start in surprise and come after her. She weaved through the couples, hoping to elude the marquis and avoid a scene.

Meanwhile, the earl found himself at the entrance to the ballroom with Betsy at his side. "Where is Angella?"

"Why do you care?" His harsh tone surprised him as much as Betsy.

Her shocked expression made him stop and take himself in hand. Whatever Angella had done, there was no reason to take out his anger and disillusionment on his cousin. She seemed to be having a good evening and he didn't wish to destroy an evening to remember. Maybe she would find an eligible *parti* tonight.

He spoke more quietly, trying not to remember the disappointment on Angella's face when he deserted her in the hall. Anger still simmered against the woman who had seemed so different when she first came to him. "I left her in the hall after her supper antics."

Betsy frowned at him. "Her antics. Looked to me like she was only doing her best to be polite to a man she doesn't care for overmuch. Angella is not one to cause a scene."

The earl frowned. Was he missing something?

Lady Carrington overheard and walked toward them. A smile touched her lips. "Jealousy does color things."

"Jealous. Have you run mad?" The earl felt his chest tighten. "I gave her a season to know her mind. Obviously, she's made that up. You both witnessed her and the marquis at supper, looking very cozy."

"Fustian!" His aunt shook her head. "She left rather precipitously. Seemed to me and many others she sought an excuse to leave him."

Betsy added, "Looked to me like she was all but running out on that awful old man." Betsy stared at her cousin. "You knew, did you not, that she doesn't care for him by half?"

"Is this true?" The earl's gaze narrowed. "How do you know this?" His stomach churned with nausea.

Betsy took his arm. "Spensor, she has been trying to avoid him, but he will not leave her alone. She told me he almost reminded her of the vicar in the village from which she came. He was very possessive." She blinked back tears. "I told her I'd help her tonight and keep him away from her, but fear I failed her. I was so caught up in actually having willing partners for a change, I didn't stay with her. Oh." She gulped back a sob. "Even I realized he watched her all evening and all but stalked her."

His aunt agreed. "So it would seem…" Her voice trailed off in distress.

Angella had compared the marquis to the vicar. For the first time the earl realized what he had said when Angella asked for his help. He left her. *Dear God, he left her.* If the marquis was like the vicar, Angella, *his Angella,* felt that she would be compromised or was being forced into a marriage she did not want. And he had given his consent. Oh, what must she think of him?

"We have to find her," he said to no one in particular. He didn't realize as he headed into the ballroom that Betsy followed.

He paid no attention to the butler, who held something out. Betsy grabbed the letters and followed. Spensor merely nodded and kept going.

As he reached the middle of the ballroom, Angella turned and barreled into his arms.

The marquis was right behind her. The earl pulled her out of the way just in time to keep the marquis from running into her. The marquis stopped dead, shocked at seeing the earl. "Ah, Lucashire—" he sought to lower his tone "—just the man I wished to see. I'm ready to take your ward off your hands."

"No!" Angella whispered in the earl's ear.

The earl held Angella close and shushed her as he faced the marquis and said quietly, "I take offense at your tone and your words. Let us all go into a private room to finish this conversation."

"A very good idea," the marquis agreed. "It is time to close the deal." He nodded with a satisfied look.

The earl herded them all into the study, including his aunt and Betsy.

He stood in front of the fireplace and turned to face the marquis. "Your marked attentions to my ward this evening have exposed her to tittle-tattle. I've heard it said more than once that there will soon be an announcement. I can't imagine where the gossipmongers got that idea, can you? Have you told anyone that my ward has agreed to marry you?"

The marquis seemed to quail under the earl's hard stare and he sputtered, "Well…she did give everyone at dinner the impression that she was not averse to my suit. And she danced more than once with me this evening."

"Only because you gave me no choice if I was to avoid making a scene," Angella spat. "Believe me, I did not dance with you because I wanted to. And I did not encourage your attentions."

The earl's expression hardened even more as he addressed the marquis. "If you think I'll give your suit any credence, think again. The lady has made it plain she declines your offer. I want you to leave immediately. Furthermore, if you speak a word of this to anyone, you will find yourself barred from White's." He paused. "Is that clear?"

The marquis ground his teeth, and the look in the man's eyes made the earl clench his fists. It was all he could do to control the urge to punch the supercilious peer. Doing so would only harm his Angella and cause them to become the latest on-dits. Something he wished to avoid at all costs.

This was Angella's special night and it had already been turned into a night she'd want to forget. It hurt to know he had contributed to making it the nightmare it had become for her. Why hadn't he listened to her? Much of this could have been avoided. What transpired was as much his fault as the marquis's. No, starting a brawl would not do, would not do at all. He had Angella to think of and that meant getting rid of the marquis as quickly as possible and rejoining their guests.

The earl all but snarled at the heavyset peer. "Get out—now."

The marquis balanced back on his heels. "Surely you don't mean…"

"Oh, I do…" This time there was no mistaking the menace in his tone or the clenched fists.

The marquis paled, finally taking the earl seriously. "I have the ear of…"

"You don't want to even consider a word against my ward. Doing so would force me to speak to those who will make life exceedingly difficult for a marquis with financial problems."

The marquis gritted his teeth. He gave a slight bow to acknowledge that Lucashire had the upper hand. He could not quite let it go. Bowing to Angella, he took her hand in his. "My dear, I fear we will not suit. I shall take my leave." He glanced toward Spensor. "Not a word will pass these lips of what has transpired. You have the word of a gentleman." With that, he released Angella's hand, turned and left them.

The earl watched the man head down the hall. "Gentleman. He doesn't know the meaning of the word." He focused on Angella. "He's gone and I…"

Angella trembled. "Oh, Spensor…he said you'd given your permission…" She burst into tears.

"He is a bounder, make no mistake."

"But you left me. You wouldn't listen." The hurt on Angella's face cut him deeply.

"Oh, Angella, I am so sorry. I've been so jealous."

She straightened. "Jealous. But I thought you were trying to get rid of me."

"Oh, my dear!" Lucashire groaned. "I owe you so much more than an apology. I fear I've destroyed everything and all because I let Margaret put doubt in my mind. With so little experience of men, how could you know your own mind? I only wanted to make sure you cared for me and me alone."

"Why throw me at all those so-called eligible partis?" Angella wiped tears from her cheeks. "And you were never around... But surely you could not imagine that I could care for such a man as that odious marquis. I don't care about his silly title. I wouldn't care if he owned half of England. He is insufferable. He would not have bothered with me if you had not settled a portion on me." Her look was accusing.

The earl bowed his head until their foreheads touched. "I wanted to give you a season and freedom to choose, but..." He raised his head, a wry grin on his lips. "I was so jealous—though, I refused to admit to it—I could not stand to see you in anyone else's arms, even an odious, insufferable marquis."

"Oh." Angella's eyes widened with understanding. "Spensor, I wish I'd known."

She watched misery take over his expression. "Have my noddy-cock actions destroyed what we had, could have had? Angella, my dear, I do love you. Every day I love you more. There were times I wanted to punch those dandies seeking your favor."

At his confession, forgiveness flooded her heart. Betsy hadn't been far wrong. Why could she not have seen it sooner? "No, all is not lost. I never stopped loving you, Spensor. I thought you..." She gulped and shook her head.

"Never. Ever. You are so lovely and pure and my life..."

"Has been washed in the blood of Christ. You are

forgiven of it all, my love." She paused. "I am so tired of the season."

"Then you'll return to Lucashire with me?"

Angella sighed and hugged him with relief. "I'd like that very much, Spensor."

"Yes, then. As soon as possible, but—" he held her close and stared into her eyes as he finished "—only as my bride, beloved."

She smiled then, a smile that lit her entire face. "Oh, Spensor." She leaned into his kiss, a kiss that was a promise not only for the present, but for a future filled with hope and love.

Through Angella's mind flashed, *Fear thou not; for I am with thee…*

God always had been with her, and always would be. Her heart sang *Thank You, Lord. Thank You.*

With that, she gave herself up to Spensor's loving embrace.

As their kiss deepened, Betsy cleared her throat. "Ah…"

Angella flushed as she looked up. "I…I didn't know you were here."

Betsy giggled nervously. "I came to help, but you two didn't need my help. I didn't know how to leave, but…" She held out the mail. "I think you'll want to see these."

Betsy winked at Angella and hugged her cousin. "About time. I'll keep quiet, but don't wait too long for the announcement." Then she was gone.

"This is your night, darling. Shall we announce our engagement tonight?"

"You really wish to marry me?"

Spensor kissed her again. "As soon as you'll have me."

"Let's make the announcement later. This night has had enough excitement, don't you agree?"

"Quite."

"And we have to finish the season, for Betsy's sake. We shouldn't cut her season short just because we're tired of it. She must have her chance."

"You're so right, my love. But we will announce our engagement soon."

Leading her to a nearby sofa done in shades of rose, he pulled her down beside him and reached for one of the letters. Opening it, he announced, "Mary had her baby. Both mother and son are doing fine. Alistair and Winter plan to be back within the week."

"I am so glad for them."

She turned over the other envelope. Inside was another letter from Edward. She gulped. She opened it, then read through it. Excitement set a smile on her lips. "Oh, Spensor. Edward has landed in England and is on his way to London. Now Edward can be part of our wedding!" She hesitated. "That is all right?"

"Very all right, my dear." He held her close.

Angella leaned against him. "God indeed is good."

"Yes, He is," agreed Spensor, as Angella melted into his arms.

* * * * *

REQUEST YOUR FREE BOOKS!

2 FREE INSPIRATIONAL NOVELS
PLUS 2
FREE
MYSTERY GIFTS

Love Inspired

YES! Please send me 2 FREE Love Inspired® novels and my 2 FREE mystery gifts (gifts are worth about $10). After receiving them, if I don't wish to receive any more books, I can return the shipping statement marked "cancel." If I don't cancel, I will receive 6 brand-new novels every month and be billed just $4.74 per book in the U.S. or $5.24 per book in Canada. That's a savings of at least 21% off the cover price. It's quite a bargain! Shipping and handling is just 50¢ per book in the U.S. and 75¢ per book in Canada.* I understand that accepting the 2 free books and gifts places me under no obligation to buy anything. I can always return a shipment and cancel at any time. Even if I never buy another book, the two free books and gifts are mine to keep forever.

105/305 IDN F49N

Name   (PLEASE PRINT)

Address   Apt. #

City   State/Prov.   Zip/Postal Code

Signature (if under 18, a parent or guardian must sign)

Mail to the Harlequin® Reader Service:
IN U.S.A.: P.O. Box 1867, Buffalo, NY 14240-1867
IN CANADA: P.O. Box 609, Fort Erie, Ontario L2A 5X3

**Are you a subscriber to Love Inspired books
and want to receive the larger-print edition?
Call 1-800-873-8635 or visit www.ReaderService.com.**

* Terms and prices subject to change without notice. Prices do not include applicable taxes. Sales tax applicable in N.Y. Canadian residents will be charged applicable taxes. Offer not valid in Quebec. This offer is limited to one order per household. Not valid for current subscribers to Love Inspired books. All orders subject to credit approval. Credit or debit balances in a customer's account(s) may be offset by any other outstanding balance owed by or to the customer. Please allow 4 to 6 weeks for delivery. Offer available while quantities last.

Your Privacy—The Harlequin® Reader Service is committed to protecting your privacy. Our Privacy Policy is available online at www.ReaderService.com or upon request from the Harlequin Reader Service.
We make a portion of our mailing list available to reputable third parties that offer products we believe may interest you. If you prefer that we not exchange your name with third parties, or if you wish to clarify or modify your communication preferences, please visit us at www.ReaderService.com/consumerchoice or write to us at Harlequin Reader Service Preference Service, P.O. Box 9062, Buffalo, NY 14269. Include your complete name and address.

LIDIR13R

REQUEST YOUR FREE BOOKS!

2 FREE INSPIRATIONAL NOVELS
PLUS 2
FREE
MYSTERY GIFTS

Love Inspired

HISTORICAL

INSPIRATIONAL HISTORICAL ROMANCE

YES! Please send me 2 FREE Love Inspired® Historical novels and my 2 FREE mystery gifts (gifts are worth about $10). After receiving them, if I don't wish to receive any more books, I can return the shipping statement marked "cancel." If I don't cancel, I will receive 4 brand-new novels every month and be billed just $4.74 per book in the U.S. or $5.24 per book in Canada. That's a savings of at least 21% off the cover price. It's quite a bargain! Shipping and handling is just 50¢ per book in the U.S. and 75¢ per book in Canada.* I understand that accepting the 2 free books and gifts places me under no obligation to buy anything. I can always return a shipment and cancel at any time. Even if I never buy another book, the two free books and gifts are mine to keep forever.

102/302 IDN F5CY

Name	(PLEASE PRINT)	
Address		Apt. #
City	State/Prov.	Zip/Postal Code

Signature (if under 18, a parent or guardian must sign)

Mail to the Harlequin® Reader Service:
IN U.S.A.: P.O. Box 1867, Buffalo, NY 14240-1867
IN CANADA: P.O. Box 609, Fort Erie, Ontario L2A 5X3

Want to try two free books from another series?
Call 1-800-873-8635 or visit www.ReaderService.com.

* Terms and prices subject to change without notice. Prices do not include applicable taxes. Sales tax applicable in N.Y. Canadian residents will be charged applicable taxes. Offer not valid in Quebec. This offer is limited to one order per household. Not valid for current subscribers to Love Inspired Historical books. All orders subject to credit approval. Credit or debit balances in a customer's account(s) may be offset by any other outstanding balance owed by or to the customer. Please allow 4 to 6 weeks for delivery. Offer available while quantities last.

Your Privacy—The Harlequin® Reader Service is committed to protecting your privacy. Our Privacy Policy is available online at www.ReaderService.com or upon request from the Harlequin Reader Service.

We make a portion of our mailing list available to reputable third parties that offer products we believe may interest you. If you prefer that we not exchange your name with third parties, or if you wish to clarify or modify your communication preferences, please visit us at www.ReaderService.com/consumerchoice or write to us at Harlequin Reader Service Preference Service, P.O. Box 9062, Buffalo, NY 14269. Include your complete name and address.

LIHDIR13R

REQUEST YOUR FREE BOOKS!
2 FREE WHOLESOME ROMANCE NOVELS IN LARGER PRINT
PLUS 2 FREE MYSTERY GIFTS

★ ★ ★ ★ ★ ★ ★ ★ ★ ★ ★ ★ ★ ★ ★ ★ ★ ★

HEARTWARMING™

❀ ❀ ❀ ❀ ❀ ❀ ❀ ❀ ❀ ❀ ❀ ❀ ❀ ❀ ❀ ❀ ❀ ❀

Wholesome, tender romances

YES! Please send me 2 FREE Harlequin® Heartwarming Larger-Print novels and my 2 FREE mystery gifts (gifts worth about $10). After receiving them, if I don't wish to receive any more books, I can return the shipping statement marked "cancel." If I don't cancel, I will receive 4 brand-new larger-print novels every month and be billed just $4.99 per book in the U.S. or $5.74 per book in Canada. That's a savings of at least 23% off the cover price. It's quite a bargain! Shipping and handling is just 50¢ per book in the U.S. and 75¢ per book in Canada.* I understand that accepting the 2 free books and gifts places me under no obligation to buy anything. I can always return a shipment and cancel at any time. Even if I never buy another book, the two free books and gifts are mine to keep forever.

161/361 IDN F47N

Name _____ (PLEASE PRINT)

Address _____ Apt. #

City _____ State/Prov. _____ Zip/Postal Code

Signature (if under 18, a parent or guardian must sign)

Mail to the **Harlequin® Reader Service:**
IN U.S.A.: P.O. Box 1867, Buffalo, NY 14240-1867
IN CANADA: P.O. Box 609, Fort Erie, Ontario L2A 5X3

* Terms and prices subject to change without notice. Prices do not include applicable taxes. Sales tax applicable in N.Y. Canadian residents will be charged applicable taxes. Offer not valid in Quebec. This offer is limited to one order per household. Not valid for current subscribers to Harlequin Heartwarming larger-print books. All orders subject to credit approval. Credit or debit balances in a customer's account(s) may be offset by any other outstanding balance owed by or to the customer. Please allow 4 to 6 weeks for delivery. Offer available while quantities last.

Your Privacy—The Harlequin® Reader Service is committed to protecting your privacy. Our Privacy Policy is available online at www.ReaderService.com or upon request from the Harlequin Reader Service.

We make a portion of our mailing list available to reputable third parties that offer products we believe may interest you. If you prefer that we not exchange your name with third parties, or if you wish to clarify or modify your communication preferences, please visit us at www.ReaderService.com/consumerschoice or write to us at Harlequin Reader Service Preference Service, P.O. Box 9062, Buffalo, NY 14269. Include your complete name and address.

HWDIR13R

ReaderService.com

Manage your account online!

- Review your order history
- Manage your payments
- Update your address

> *We've designed the Harlequin® Reader Service website just for you.*

Enjoy all the features!

- Reader excerpts from any series
- Respond to mailings and special monthly offers
- Discover new series available to you
- Browse the Bonus Bucks catalog
- Share your feedback

Visit us at:
ReaderService.com